ASSASSINATION
AT HIGH SPEED

RICHARD BALDWIN

This novel is a product of the author's imagination. The events described in this story never occurred. Though localities, buildings, and businesses may exist, liberties were taken with their actual location and description. This story has no purpose other than to entertain the reader.

Published by Buttonwood Press
P.O. Box 716
Haslett, Michigan 48840
www.buttonwoodpress.com

ISBN: 978-0-9823351-4-7
Printed in the United States of America

*This book is dedicated
to train enthusiasts of all ages.
Had I not been given
a Lionel set as a youngster,
I may not have grown up
enjoying trains.*

OTHER BOOKS
BY RICHARD L. BALDWIN

FICTION:

A Lesson Plan for Murder (1998)
ISBN: 0-9660685-0-5. Buttonwood Press.

The Principal Cause of Death (1999)
ISBN: 0-9660685-2-1. Buttonwood Press.

Administration Can Be Murder (2000)
ISBN: 0-9660685-4-8. Buttonwood Press.

Buried Secrets of Bois Blanc: Murder in the Straits of Mackinac (2001)
ISBN: 0-9660685-5-6. Buttonwood Press.

The Marina Murders (2003)
ISBN: 0-9660685-7-2. Buttonwood Press.

A Final Crossing: Murder on the S.S. Badger (2004)
ISBN: 0-9742920-2-8. Buttonwood Press.

Poaching Man and Beast: Murder in the North Woods (2006)
ISBN: 0-9742920-3-6. Buttonwood Press.

The Lighthouse Murders (2007)
ISBN: 978-0-9742920-5-2. Buttonwood Press.

Murder in Thin Air (2008)
ISBN: 978-0-9742920-9-0. Buttonwood Press.

Murder at the Ingham County Fair (2009)
ISBN: 978-0-9823351-0-9. Buttonwood Press.

Murder in Tip-Up Town (2010)

ISBN: 978-0-9823351-2-3. Buttonwood Press.

The Searing Mysteries: Three in One (2001)

ISBN: 0-9660685-6-4. Buttonwood Press.

The Moon Beach Mysteries (2003)

ISBN: 0-9660685-9-9. Buttonwood Press.

The Detective Company (2004; written with Sandie Jones.)

ISBN: 0-9742920-0-1. Buttonwood Press.

SPIRITUAL:

Unity and the Children (2000)

ISBN: 0-9660685-3-X. Buttonwood Press.

NON-FICTION:

The Piano Recital (1999)

ISBN: 0-9660685-1-3. Buttonwood Press.

A Story to Tell: Special Education in Michigan's Upper Peninsula 1902-1975 (1994)

ISBN: 932212-77-8. Lake Superior Press.

Warriors and Special Olympics: The Wertz Warrior Story (2006)

ISBN: 0-9742920-4-4. Buttonwood Press, LLC.

ACKNOWLEDGEMENTS

I want to thank the Buttonwood Press team: editor, Anne Ordiway; proofreader, Joyce Wagner; cover designer/typesetter, Sarah Thomas, and webmaster, Heidi Roberts. Others who helped by answering questions and/or offering advice pertaining to certain aspects of the story include Robert Strobel, Don Hibbard, Bill Gohier, Carolyn Soloman, Dave Kirk, Joe Bixler, Byron Rogers, and Kaye Distelrath. Thank you all.

Finally, I wish to thank my dear wife Patty for her belief in me, her love and support. I am so blessed to share life with the most beautiful human being on the face of the earth.

PROLOGUE

The Michigan Congressional delegation had negotiated for months with the Canadian Prime Minister, the U.S. President, and the Chairs of the Transportation Committees in the U.S. House and Senate regarding the creation of a speed rail system in the Midwest. Similar efforts had arisen along the eastern seaboard, but there were no incentives or plans for high-speed travel in the Midwest. Given the huge government debt, high-speed rail programs seemed to hold the same priority as burnt toast. But the President was determined to have something to show for his vision and, contrary to popular perception, a high-speed rail system was determined to be a potential economic windfall for Michigan.

The Canadian Prime Minister had originally wanted a high-speed rail system that would cross his country, but he was convinced that if U.S. federal and state legislation could be passed, he could work out the "kinks," by joining with the States in creating a rail system from Toronto to Sarnia.

Then Michigan would extend the service from Port Huron to New Buffalo, and Indiana and Illinois would complete the line to Chicago.

Legislation was introduced in the House by a mid-Michigan representative and shortly thereafter introduced in the Senate. The legislation would require the successful bidding state or states to match the federal contribution and for Canada to pay for its section of the route. The legislation passed unanimously in both chambers and was signed by the President.

Three states eagerly bid on the multi-billion dollar package: Michigan; Missouri, with a proposed route between St. Louis and Kansas City; and a joint venture between Minnesota and Wisconsin for a Milwaukee to Minneapolis route.

Michigan was awarded the contract after a bitter fight, each state lobbying and spending millions to convince federal officials that its proposal would be the most beneficial for America. Missouri came in second, and the Minnesota and Wisconsin proposal finished a distant third.

To celebrate this coup, the Governor of Michigan planned that the President and the Prime Minister would join him on a Victory Ride from Port Huron to New Buffalo on Amtrak's Blue Water Limited. Celebrations were planned at the current stops of Port Huron, Lapeer, Flint, East Lansing, Battle Creek, Kalamazoo, Dowagiac, Niles, and New Buffalo so the citizens could express their appreciation for an initiative that might very well put Michigan on the economic track, as it were.

Unfortunately, the policy decision met strong opposition in the United States and especially in Canada, where nationalists were furious with the Prime Minister's support of a token project in southern Ontario. Neither the President nor the Prime Minister was popular for his support of the high-speed rail. Opposition for both men was high-pitched and the usual round of death threats doubled. The Victory Ride would be an effort to restore some of their popularity.

CHAPTER ONE

On April 2, President Alan Fortner convened a meeting with Marcia Ludlow, Head of Homeland Security; Willard Caruthers, his Chief of Staff; Dr. Spoelman, his personal physician; and Robert Singleton, Director of the FBI. He had requested coffee and sweet rolls because Marcia was much more likely to go along with a plan with a sweet roll in one hand and a hot cup of coffee in the other.

The President began, "I'd like to discuss my upcoming trip to Michigan for their Victory Ride. Rollie Halloran, Michigan's Governor, has asked me to spend a day with him and Canadian Prime Minister Leon Abernathy aboard Amtrak's Blue Water Limited, a rail route between Port Huron and New Buffalo."

"You plan to ride a train for a day?" Marcia Ludlow asked, a tinge of disbelief in her voice. "Going to Port Huron to kick it off, yes. But do you really intend to spend all day on a train?"

"Yes, I do."

"Mr. President, security efforts will be particularly difficult to coordinate," Marcia emphasized.

"I realize that; the purpose of this meeting is to go over the modified security plans," President Fortner stated firmly, passing the donuts to Ms. Ludlow.

"I assume this 'Victory Ride' will stop along the way for you to speak?" Marcia asked, accepting the donuts and choosing a chocolate covered one.

"That's correct."

"Mr. President, I feel very strongly that we can't protect you in the manner you expect if you spend a full day on a train, getting on and off several times." It was rare that Marcia stood up to the President, but he had just presented his Director of Homeland Security with a very difficult task.

"Then I suggest you and your staff get to work on it. I am making the trip," President Fortner replied, unsmiling. "The American people should see the President traveling on an Amtrak train just like any other citizen."

"That may have been the case previously, but given the continuing terrorism, we can't allow you to be that visible in so many places, especially confined to a rail car," Marcia countered.

"As I said, put your heads together and give me a plan," the President repeated, his jaw set.

"Yes, Mr. President."

President Fortner turned to Dr. Spoelman, his physician. "What will you need on this trip?"

"I'd like a train car and at least a day to equip it before the trip," replied the physician.

"Do I really need a hospital on the train?" President Fortner asked.

"I need to be ready for anything, sir. I'll also need a list of every hospital along the route."

"That shouldn't be difficult."

"On the surface, I agree, but I need to know which hospitals are equipped to treat trauma. If the train is going through rural areas, my guess is that most don't have such facilities or skilled physicians to meet every medical need."

"I think I'll just enjoy a day on the train and take my chances that nothing requires more than an aspirin," the President remarked, annoyed at such extravagant procedures.

"I can't allow it, sir," Marcia stated. "I have an obligation to the American public that you receive the finest medical care possible."

President Fortner turned to Mr. Singleton. "Are you aware of any persons or issues that would make me more vulnerable in Michigan?"

"You mean other than the regular daily round of threats on your life?"

"Exactly."

"We don't know of any specific threats," Robert replied. "Of course, even with the best surveillance, a surprise attack is always possible."

"I realize that, but should any radical group in Michigan give me pause at being out in public?"

"Not that I know of, sir."

"How about communications?" President Fortner asked.

"Barring a nationwide electrical failure, a computer virus, or a disruption of a magnitude to block communication, you'll keep in touch with your staff here at the White House."

"Looks like we've got that covered," President Fortner remarked. He turned to his Chief of Staff, Willard Caruthers, "Tell me about travel plans. I assume I'll fly into Selfridge Air Force Base and have a fleet of limos for the trip to Port Huron?"

"Yes."

"The next evening, I leave on Air Force One from South Bend. Correct?"

"That's right."

"Where will my limo be during the trip?" the President asked.

"Your limo will take you from the Thomas Edison Inn to the Amtrak station. Once you board the Victory Ride, your limo will head to Niles. When you finish in New Buffalo at the end of the day, you'll be driven to the South Bend airport and then fly to D.C."

"So, I will stay at the Edison Inn the night before the ride?"

"That's correct," Willard replied. "Marcia's staff has already made arrangements there."

President Fortner turned to his social secretary, Amy Poole, "Anything else I need to know at this point?"

"Protocols must be followed. You will have a reception at the Edison Inn for party leaders from Michigan. Thomas Edison is the most famous person to walk the town to date. As a boy he sold papers on a train going to Detroit to get money to buy supplies and equipment for his laboratory. You'll be in second place, Mr. President, but with enough smiles and photo ops, you might move into first place."

"That's farthest from my mind," President Fortner replied, smiling. "Let Mr. Edison retain his place in history. I'm just in town for a night."

The President turned to his speech-writer, Terry Adams. "You know all about the Victory Ride—what it is, why I am going?"

"Yes. I've completed first drafts of your speeches."

"Good. They can be basically the same for each stop, but I want to mention something unique about the town where I'm speaking."

"Yes, sir," Terry replied. "I've got it covered."

"In East Lansing I'll want to say something about Michigan State University, and in Kalamazoo, about Western Michigan University."

"Sports, sir?" Terry asked.

"Yes, include something about their spring teams—how their baseball, tennis, and golf teams are doing. In East Lansing

I'll mention the cyclotron, and their new art museum. In Kalamazoo I'll want to tout Western's Speech and Audiology Department, programs in the arts, and teacher education."

CHAPTER TWO

On April 26 at 6:30 a.m., the Blue Water Limited was ready for the Victory Ride from Port Huron to Chicago on the Grand Trunk Rail System. This one-day celebration had been planned for months. The weather was absolutely gorgeous, the epitome of an early spring day. Aboard would be Michigan's Governor, Roland Halloran; Canada's Prime Minister, Leon Abernathy; and the President of the United States, Alan Fortner.

The locomotive was draped with patriotic bunting—red, white and blue for the United States, red and white for Canada. Michigan, Canada, and U.S. flags fluttered from short poles at the front of the locomotive. Every train car had been washed and polished. In fact, citizens along the Blue Water Limited would be seeing the cleanest train ever to cross Michigan.

The engineer was Larry Fitzpatrick. He had been briefed by federal security agents—the entire line was his. For security purposes, there would be no other trains on the route. Ahead of the engine would be a pickup truck with adaptive train wheels, the purpose of which was to secure the route and check overpasses, trestles, and entrances to planned stops along the way. Larry would be joined in the cab by a member of the Secret Service.

One car on the train was for the media, one for technology, one for medical purposes, one for security, and one more carried food and drink. Finally, a sixth car was turned into a makeshift office for the Prime Minister and the President. All of the train's windows had been replaced with bullet-proof glass and its doors with thick steel-reinforced doors. A few "dummy" cars were added to lessen the possibility that people could tell exactly where the President, Prime Minister, and Governor were riding.

As the sun rose higher and the crowd grew, the Governor, Prime Minister, and the President waited for their cue to offer comments. Floodlights from all the major networks showered light onto a podium adorned with U.S. and Canadian flags positioned on either side of the microphones. A crowd of about two thousand had gathered at the Port Huron station for the send-off. On cue, a high school band played the *Star Spangled Banner,* and *O Canada* as school children held flags aloft.

Matt Lauer of NBC's *Today Show* broke into the early morning festivities, "While the country warms its coffee, a train tour across southern Michigan is about to begin, bringing international attention to a new speed-rail system that will carry Michigan and Ontario into the futuristic world of high-speed transportation. The Governor of Michigan, Roland Halloran, is about to speak."

The Governor approached the podium. "President Fortner, Prime Minister Abernathy, dignitaries and guests. Welcome to Michigan! Our motto is: 'If you seek a pleasant peninsula, look about you.' You are in a state whose citizens are struggling out of a horrendous economic recession. We were the center of the automobile industry and a vibrant economy once surrounded our manufacturing Great Lake State.

"The United States is a bit late in leaving the station— pun intended—but we are eager to join Japan and Europe in providing safe, fast, and economical transportation. I wish to thank the citizens of the State of Michigan and our Canadian neighbors for their cooperation in this adventure. Our countries have worked together on a number of initiatives, but this one will change the transportation system of the Midwest.

"Presently, we will lead the nation and the world in a resurrected economy based on speed. My staff has distributed a report in which is summarized the future of this enterprise and what it will mean to the Midwest and to our Canadian neighbors. In summary, it means jobs for citizens of both countries. But for now, let me welcome you to what will become a new Michigan, and to the future of high-speed rail transportation in the Province of Ontario and America!"

Roland glanced at the Prime Minister. "This morning the President and I thank you, Mr. Abernathy, for showing the world that two countries can work together to create jobs and a transportation system equal to none in the world."

Back in New York, Lauer said, "We've obtained a copy of the report Governor Halloran referenced a moment ago. It is impressive to say the least. The report is quite technical and full of financial plans and goals, but what jumps off the page is a vision of progress, innovation, and a sustained industry based on speed. Canada's Prime Minister, Leon Abernathy, is about to speak. Let's go back to Port Huron."

"Good morning. The people of Canada join me in extending a hand of friendship to our neighbors in Michigan and to the Government of the United States. We are eager to begin construction on the high-speed rail system in North America. I can assure all who hear me that once this section of high-speed rail is complete, we will take all we have learned and span Canada, from the Pacific Northwest to our eastern-most province. I'm sure the United States will span its territory with the same innovative rail system. Your Canadian neighbors join you on your Victory Ride!" The crowd cheered.

Governor Halloran stepped forward again. "It is my privilege and honor to introduce the man who has made this day possible. While Congress and most Americans fail to see the enormous benefit of high-speed rail, our President has a vision. And most importantly, he wants to see Michigan rise from deep recession to a glorious future. He believes that a state which held world prominence in automobile manufacturing can do the same with a high-speed rail system. This man believes in us and in our State. Ladies and gentlemen, I present to you, the leader of the free world, the President of the United States, the Honorable Alan Fortner."

While the Port Huron High School band played *Hail to the Chief,* the President emerged from the railroad car and made his way to the podium while the crowd gave him a sustained and enthusiastic welcome.

"Thank you, Governor Halloran. Good morning, my friends. This truly is a good morning for the citizens of Michigan and for all of the United States. Michigan has committed to a great economic future. The infrastructure for the high-speed rail system is already in place as current rail networks can be adapted to this high-speed system. I fear, Mr. Governor, that once this is up and running, passengers will experience your pleasant peninsula as a blur. It was my pleasure to work with your senators and several of your representatives to shepherd this through the Congress. We're about to ride across Michigan, bringing good news at each stop. Thanks for coming out for our early departure."

The three leaders stood together for several minutes for photos. As handshakes were offered and the dignitaries waved to the crowd, the conductor's traditional shout permeated the crisp morning air: "All aboard!" With that, the train slowly pulled out of the station while the crowd cheered.

At first blush it appeared that the benefits to Michigan and the Midwest were a no-brainer. Futurists predicted a resurgence of jobs in research, engineering and design, and of course, diverse manufacturing. But, as with any change, there was opposition. For every supporter of a new concept, there is an opposing force. In this case, three major lobbyists, as well as the Chamber of Commerce of Michigan were opposed to creation of this innovative high-speed rail system.

One lobbyist, representing the Teamsters Union, considered high-speed trains a threat to the trucking industry. The Air Transportation Union lobbyist maintained the rail system threatened airlines business, for people could get to Michigan cities and to Chicago faster and without the airport hassles. The third lobbyist represented the Michigan Congress for Reduced Government, who opposed the rail-line on principle. The Chamber was concerned because many cities along the way would lose stops, as the agreement allowed for only three on the route: Lapeer, East Lansing, and Kalamazoo. Many Chamber members would lose the novelty of the train stopping in their community. Their quaint stations, many containing relics and memorabilia of the past, would yield to a future of high-speed technology. The people of Durand were particularly upset—they prided themselves on being a railroad town, complete with a museum and a lot of people who enjoyed the railroad.

To win this competition in the nation's capitol, the Michigan Legislature was required to offer a sizeable contribution, and the dollars were simply not yet in the general fund. Many citizens questioned the required increase in taxes simply to go faster from Point A to Point B. Leading economists readily admitted the state would realize the long-term benefits of this system and its accompanying construction and implementation, but reasons for opposition to this initiative were obvious.

The lobbyists met regularly in Lansing as the legislation moved from committee hearings to the floor of the Michigan House and Senate. Eventually they saw that the legislation would pass by a narrow margin because of the billions promised by the automakers as thanks to the President and Congress for the bail-out they received a few years ago. Willing to admit partial defeat, lobbyists began to focus on preventing the system from getting on the rails. Quite simply, the lobbyists had failed the first test, but each person feared members within their unions might take matters into their own hands.

Many Canadians also protested the high-speed rail decision. The print media were more critical than citizens, but it wasn't clear whether editors were protesting Prime Minister Abernathy's decisions or whether they believed the decision was bad for the Canadian people. Nonetheless, newspapers and the visual media were having a field day denouncing the plan and encouraging opposition demonstrations.

At a particularly alarming demonstration in Montreal, three stickmen labeled "Rollie," "Alan," and "Leon" were burned, along with numerous signs, one of which read, "Make Decisions for the People, Not for Politics!" Montreal police were concerned the mob might turn violent and storm Parliament, but Royal Canadian Mounted Police (RCMP) officers on horseback and threats of tear gas eventually dispersed the crowd.

Letters to editors of all major Canadian papers denounced the demonstration, saying protests should be carried out at the ballot box and not on the streets of Canada. One headline, "Canada Embarrassed by Bullies!" seemed to hit the nail on the head. People finally figured out that the government had bigger fish to fry than a hundred-mile strip of railroad and lost interest in the issue. Or, at least the majority of people angered by Mr. Abernathy's agreement with the Government of the United States became less vocal.

CHAPTER THREE

Lou Searing, private investigator from Grand Haven, had traditional earmarks of someone seventy years old: male-pattern baldness, a slight belly from too much chocolate, two hearing aids from a youthful bout with the measles, and a pair of bifocals to see up close and far away.

Following years in special education as a teacher, university professor, and government worker in the Michigan Department of Education, Lou retired in 1997. He found a second career when he discovered a talent for solving difficult murders; he single-handedly solved the murder of a close friend in the mid-1990s. Most people were astonished that he was able to find the facts to complete his work.

He seemed to be living a charmed life with his wife Carol and their dog Samm. They lived in a beautiful home the Searings had built in the dunes south of Grand Haven, a gift to each other when they both retired from jobs in special education.

Lou's writing studio and Carol's quilting studio were on the second floor.

Over the years, Lou's reputation grew in stature. He was welcomed into most law enforcement agencies to help solve a murder. Lou would tell you that luck plays a huge role in crime-solving, to say nothing of the help he had received from Maggie McMillan in his earliest investigations and now gained from Jack Kelly of Muskegon. While Lou was popular with law enforcement, he was better known to the public for the books he wrote about the cases he solved—written under the pen name Richard L. Baldwin, a boyhood friend.

On April 26, 1957, Lou hit a hole-in-one on the then 11th hole at the Spring Lake Country Club. The unexpected event occurred during his first high school varsity golf match as a sophomore at Grand Haven High School. So, each year Lou returned to the Country Club to relive the moment and see if he was lucky enough to recreate the feat. After 54 years of playing the 11th hole, the closest he'd ever come to the cup was four inches in 1997.

Although an April day in Michigan can offer a warm day of spring or a late blast of winter, it didn't matter. The day was a memory and a fun event. Playing with Lou this year was his partner in that 1957 match against Holland High School, Jerome Kazmanski.

As Lou was about to take a cut at the Titleist golf ball on the 11th tee, his cell phone, set on vibrate, began its rhythmic pulse. Thinking it could be Carol, he told Kaz he needed to take the call.

"Hello."

"Lou, this is Larry Hicks in the Attorney General's office in Lansing."

"Yes, Larry. This better not upset me—I'm all psyched up to hit my Titleist 4 into the cup in Spring Lake."

"Sorry, Lou, but the Governor's Office directed me to call. His office received a phone threat to blow up an Amtrak train somewhere between Port Huron and Chicago."

"I take it this is about the politicians' ride to promote the speed train across Michigan?" Lou asked, seeking clarification. "I saw that on the *Today Show* this morning when I was lacing up my golf shoes in the country club locker room."

"That's right. The FBI advised that the train stop to keep everyone safe, but Governor Halloran thinks we should not give in to the threat. His office gets a few of these calls a month, and he thinks this is just another crank. He wants the Victory Ride to continue as planned. However, he did request that you become involved. Normally the State Police would handle it, but the Governor has asked Colonel Cellar, head of the State Police, to allow you to work with them."

Lou sighed, "Sounds like I need to get to that train."

"He'd appreciate it, sir."

"Well, I'll take a golf swing, finish up here, and then head to a station on the route after stopping at my home. Fax me the Amtrak schedule so I know where to get on. I'll need permission for my assistant, Jack Kelly, and me to board. And give me the number to reach the State Police on my way to meet the train."

"I'll take care of that, Lou."

"Tell the Governor I'm more than pleased to help. Between you and me, he should have listened to the FBI and called it off. I have a sense this isn't a crank call."

"I agree, but it's not my decision to make."

Lou put his phone away and said to Kaz, "Well, I'm sorry, my friend, but I need to leave after I take this shot."

"Not a problem," Kaz said, looking to the sky. "Looks like some rain off to the west. Take your shot and go where you need to go."

Lou took out a six-iron for the reenactment. He'd used a seven-iron for the hole-in-one, but at age 70, he couldn't hit a seven-iron one hundred and fifty seven yards. He placed the club behind the ball, took a deep breath, began to draw the club back and felt his phone vibrate again. He stopped in mid-swing to take the call which was a follow-up from Lansing. Lou listened as Larry Hicks provided him with the exact words of the threat: "Michigan was in the national news this morning because of the Victory Ride. Michigan will be in the national news again tonight because the Victory Ride will be the final hurrah for its passengers. This is not a hoax. I am calling because it is the right thing to do. Justice cannot be served with the violence that will affect those on the Victory Ride.

As the train sped along toward Lapeer, Governor Halloran called the leaders and their staffs together in the VIP car.

"I've received a threat that involves all of us. The caller said this trip would be the 'final hurrah' for passengers on the Victory Ride. I told my staff to check out the threat like any other, but that we would be proceeding. However, I felt an obligation to inform you because you may prefer to avoid this possibly dangerous journey. After all, they are your lives."

"I take any threat seriously," President Fortner said. "I don't want to throw a wet blanket on this celebration, but Marcia Ludlow of Homeland Security will likely demand that I get off."

"Whose decision is that to make, Mr. President?" Roland asked.

"Mine, but I respect my staff and their advice. However, I feel strongly about this day in Michigan. I believe the President needs to share good news with the American people, so I'll stay with the train."

"I understand. But we don't know where the threat came from, nor when the event may occur; nor do we know what the threat may be—bomb, shooting, or whatever." Roland was concerned. "One of us getting off might inadvertently trigger whatever is planned. We all know that 99% of these calls are simply to get attention."

"Yes, and I certainly don't want my leaving the train to trigger a catastrophe," President Fortner said. "Maybe it would be best to continue. I'll check with security to see what they recommend."

"What about you, Mr. Prime Minister? What are you thinking?" Roland asked.

"Something could happen," Leon Abernathy began. "I'm not psychic but I sometimes can sense a disaster. The threat may have come from my country, not yours, and I don't think this is the act of one person."

"In other words, our response to the threat will—or I should say, may—trigger the crisis," Roland replied.

"That's my feeling, for what it's worth," the Prime Minister shrugged.

"Your feeling?" Roland asked. "Do you know something we don't, to have these thoughts?" President Fortner asked.

"About a year ago, when we were discussing this project, I held a news conference to bring our citizens into the process. Before the press conference, security confiscated a gun from a woman who had obtained press credentials. She was arrested, and that's the last I heard. I was told that the woman was not from the media but I wonder if that episode and this threat are connected."

Once again Lou drew the six-iron away from the ball majestically sitting on a white tee on the 11th hole. He brought the club down in a perfect arc, hit the ball and some turf.

"You're on line," Kaz said quietly, not wanting to jinx the effort. Lou felt good about the shot, but whether the ball would find the cup on the right side of the green was anybody's guess. The ball landed on the green and rolled toward the cup, but as in the 54 previous years, it failed to drop.

"Another year, another miss. But, oh, how I love the memories, Kaz," Lou said with a smile.

"You were in a state of pure joy that day, Lou. What was your final score? I'm curious what effect the adrenaline flowing through your veins had on the rest of the match."

"I think I ballooned up into the early '90s. I just couldn't get over that hole-in-one. In fact, I'm not sure my feet even touched the turf for the rest of the match."

"I recall we won that match," Kaz added.

"If so, we did it without help from me," Lou replied. "It was a personal victory, and I was all wrapped up in myself. I wasn't much of a team guy that afternoon."

"Great memory."

"Well, the anniversary shot is history. I need to start on a case," Lou said. "You said you were calling it a day, right?"

"Yes. I want to beat that rain home."

Returning to the clubhouse, the men reported Lou's failed attempt to club members gathered in the pro shop, then left— Kaz to Fruitport, and Lou to Grand Haven.

Lou called his assistant Jack Kelly in Muskegon. Jack had been his right hand man for the past several investigations. He was 64, tall, slim, a handsome man with a full head of hair and a neatly-trimmed moustache.

"Hi, Elaine, is Jack home?"

"Yes, he is, Lou. Are you planning on taking him away from me again?"

"Probably."

"Well, here he is."

Elaine handed the phone to Jack, saying, "It's Lou."

"Hi, Lou. I'm ready to get to work," Jack said, excitement in his voice. "Where's the murder this time?"

"We don't have one yet, Jack. But we have a threat, and if it materializes, it could affect many people."

"So, we have no clues and nothing to solve," Jack replied. "That's more difficult than a murder investigation."

"That's right. We are being called upon to prevent a crime."

"Got it. What do you need me to do?" Jack asked.

"Get on the train."

"What train? Where and when?"

"Flint or Durand. The Victory Ride is a train trip from Port Huron to New Buffalo, with the Governor, President, and Canada's Prime Minister on board. At each stop, the mayor of the city will give a speech, the high school band will play a few numbers, the Governor will comment and introduce the dignitaries. You need to leave now. We can continue to chat on the phone. The expected time for the train to be in Durand is around 11:00 this morning."

"I've heard about the Victory Ride. Flint will take lots of open highway, Lou."

"You'll make it. If not, catch it in Durand. Don't drive recklessly or too far above the speed limit, Jack, but get there as soon as you can."

"I'm on my way. Check in with me soon, Lou."

"Will do."

Colonel Richard Cellar, State Police Commander, along with Captain Pierre DeSales, a high-ranking law enforcement official from the Ontario Provincial Police, and Marcia Ludlow, of the Department of Homeland Security, sat in the security car.

"One option is to immediately cancel the Victory Ride and get the dignitaries off the train," Marcia remarked. "That's my first response to the threat."

"That makes sense, but the Governor will not go for it," said Colonel Cellar. "The Governor has stood up to every threat in his career and, true to his belief, they've all been hot air."

"If they don't get off the train, we will have to invoke emergency procedures at each town along the route," Marcia said.

"Yes, we could do that, but Michigan would seem like a police state," Colonel Cellar replied. "The media and the crowd would not see the dignitaries, and SWAT teams will be visible. There would be no speeches where candidates were visible to the public. That would be like cancelling the Ride; security would be so tight, nothing noteworthy would happen outside the train."

"I guess we could simply proceed as planned despite the threat," Pierre offered, though he was sure his thought would be discounted.

"However, if we do that and the threat materializes, we look incompetent for not taking action to protect our leaders," Marcia replied.

"I asked Larry Hicks in the Attorney General's office to contact Lou Searing at the Governor's request," Colonel Cellar said. "Lou said he would become involved. His assistant is on his way to Flint to board the train."

Marcia was astonished. "You can't be serious!"

"I'm not kidding. Searing is legendary in Michigan. He has solved every case he's taken on, and justice is served."

"Sounds like Superman," Marcia replied with a snort.

"Well, in a sense he is. He is respected by law enforcement. He gets whatever resources he needs while solving a crime. He doesn't make us look bad. He solves the crime, and then he writes a book about the case."

"Well, if the Governor wants him involved, fine, but it's a waste of energy to me," Marcia replied. "I'm appalled that a private investigator might have any positive role in stabilizing the threat. I've yet to find anyone who can do a better job than we can with our technology and resources."

"We'll see what happens," Col. Cellar replied. "I think we owe it to the Governor to allow Mr. Searing to assist."

"Fine. If that's what you want," Marcia said, deciding not to make an issue of the civilian invading her territory.

"I agree," Pierre said, nodding.

As the Victory Ride rumbled toward Lapeer, a Canadian Air Force F-14 was getting an inspection at the Warrior Air Base in Winnipeg, Manitoba. Its pilot, Col. Ralph Stocker, was preparing for a training mission that would take the plane into U.S. air space. It was a routine mission and with open and friendly relations between the two countries, military requests to fly over each other's country were usually granted.

The training flight was a practice scramble to Toronto in the event that the city was attacked. Such exercises were scheduled regularly. Pilots and crews need flying hours, and the military couldn't practice enough in response to potential terrorist threats.

On this trip, Col. Stocker would be accompanied by a member of the Winnipeg media. Pundits believed the Canadian people needed assurance that the Provincial Government, and the country as a whole, was adequately protecting them and so a feature about the scramble would be assuring.

The reporter was Shelly Westbrook. Shelly was relatively new to the Winnipeg Free Press. She had been transferred without explanation from Ottawa to Winnipeg, a move she thought equal to a Moscow journalist being sent to Siberia. Shelly was a most attractive 38 year old woman. She was tall, dressed fashionably, had long light brown hair, and she wore a ring on each finger.

Winnipeg was a beautiful city in the heart of Manitoba, but Shelly's assignment there did not indicate she was on her way up.

She was not happy and considered retiring early, but she needed the money to support her ailing mother so she had moved west with a negative attitude.

CHAPTER FOUR

At 8:07 a.m. the Victory Ride pulled into the station in Lapeer, Michigan. The city council had pulled out all the stops to showcase their community. The mayor, Susan Grimes, had urged citizens and school children to come to the train station to see the President, the Governor of Michigan, and the Canadian Prime Minister. This was truly a historical day for Lapeer. The high school band was in formation as the train pulled to a stop. There was a brief pause while steps and a podium were placed alongside the train.

The high school band played the *Stars and Stripes Forever* with enthusiasm. School girls waited with roses to present to the dignitaries. Cheerleaders added to the excitement as the public's anticipation of this historic visit increased.

Looking out of a downtown window with a direct view of the train station was Les Trousard, a sharpshooter. Les was a man in his mid-forties who only found peace while fishing. He had never been able to please his parents, teachers, or anyone in authority. He was married for a short time in his early twenties, but the union had no chance of lasting because marriage involves giving and taking, and all Les could do was take.

Les and his fishing buddy of twenty-odd years, Randal Beaver, had been fishing in Manitoba, Canada ten years ago when a storm blew up and their boat capsized. There was no one around and the two clung to their boat for hours. As darkness enveloped the lake, they could see a light on the far shore. The two men shouted and apparently were heard, because soon after an outdoorsman arrived in a motorboat and hauled them to safety.

There was no question in anyone's mind that had not the rescuer, Mr. Houchins heard faint cries for help, Les and Randy would have died in the water. After drying off, getting clean clothes and some hot soup, Les said to Mr. Houchins, "If there's ever anything I can do for you, all you have to do is ask, and I'll do it. That's the least I could do for you. I mean, I owe my life to you, man."

At the time of the dramatic rescue, Mr. Houchins was an up-and-coming young officer in the Royal Canadian Mounted Police, stationed in Winnipeg. He was married and was the proud father of a handsome boy, Harry, and a cute girl, Heidi.

The hero's best friend was a fellow officer whose goal was to become a politician. His friend was Leon Abernathy. The two couples got together often and enjoyed a warm friendship, but Leon's advances toward the Mr. Houchins' wife were beyond what was acceptable behavior. He called Leon on it and was told, "Relax! She's like a little sister. But, if you need me to be cold, I will be. I'm sorry, man."

Now, Les found himself about to murder the Prime Minister of Canada. The culmination of the only sincere promise he'd ever made in his life—and intended to keep. While Les and Randy had never expected their rescuer to make that kind of request, it was made by someone who had saved their lives, and they would honor the request, no matter the consequences.

Les was resourceful enough to find the exact dimensions of the grandstand and the podium. The train would stop so the speakers could emerge and walk up four steps, then over to a podium where a bank of microphones was ready to capture and broadcast their words.

Les had rigged the rifle so that it would fire when he pointed a remote device toward the window, which had been raised. The rifle was clean of prints; it had been purchased from a hunter in northern Canada so law enforcement could not trace the weapon to Les.

Now, Les's instructions were to monitor the movements of the Prime Minister and when the bullet's trajectory aligned with the Prime Minister's heart, he was to point the remote at the window above and across the street from the Amtrak station. The electrical signal would fire the rifle, and if he had measured everything perfectly, the Prime Minister would never know what hit him.

Les was sure it was impossible that anyone would suspect him. He would simply watch all of the commotion and then disappear into the crowd.

The door to the train car opened and out stepped Mayor Grimes. "Welcome, welcome, my friends! What a historical and magical day this is for us." The crowd cheered. "It is my pleasure to introduce to you the Governor of Michigan, the man with a vision of jobs for Michigan. Please give a big Lapeer greeting to our Governor, Roland Halloran!"

The Governor stepped out of the train onto the platform and stood before the microphone, enjoying the warm applause. "Thank you, my friends. This is indeed a historical day. We are calling our trip the Victory Ride, because it is truly a victory— for our state, and for the entire country. We'll reap benefits from high-speed rail technology that neither you nor I can imagine. If you haven't already heard, the high-speed train—to be called "The Michigan Bullet"—will stop in Lapeer. Only two other cities have been chosen for stops." Once again the crowd cheered.

"It is now my pleasure to introduce your President, Alan Fortner. We couldn't have gotten this high-speed rail contract without the President's support. Ladies and gentlemen, our friend and your President, the Honorable Alan Fortner."

The President enjoyed the applause and the "Welcome to Lapeer, Mr. President!" banner.

"Thank you, thank you, my fellow Americans. This is a very special day for all of the United States. We're ushering in a new era. Your state, known for automobiles for more than a century, is about to begin a period of growth in rapid transportation. I am happy to be with you in Lapeer, a progressive, rural town, where people believe in the American Dream—the opportunity for all to own a home, have a job, and to raise children in a safe and vibrant community.

"We've a long day ahead, so I will now present the Prime Minister of our neighboring country of Canada, the Honorable Leon Abernathy."

The Prime Minister walked onto the platform, waving, and approached the podium. As he was about to speak, Les, out of sight of the crowd, turned, pointed the remote device toward the window, took a deep breath, and pushed the button. The high-powered rifle fired, unheard because of a silencer. As he turned, he saw the Prime Minister grimace and clutch his upper right arm. Immediately he turned away from the podium and made his way to the train car, obviously in pain.

The Prime Minister's team moved him into the medical car to assess his injury. Security personnel instantly went into crowd-control mode. The majority of the crowd, including the media contingent, assumed he had forgotten something and had gone back into the train to get it. News of the shooting actually came from media reps aboard the train.

Within a minute, an aide stepped up to the microphones, asked for attention, and then said, "Prime Minister Abernathy is fine. He experienced a sharp pain in his upper right arm, which he took to be a symptom of a heart attack, and immediately went into the train. He is being attended by his physicians. Preliminary indications are that he did not have a heart attack; perhaps it was a bee sting. We will report further as soon as details are available. Thank you for coming today."

Once the aide was safely inside, the train door was secured, and the train pulled away from the station, leaving everyone to wonder what the flurry of activity was all about. However, they had seen the dignitaries and the event was deemed a success. They would have to wait for the media to explain what had really happened.

Out of sight of the large crowd, just before the train moved, state troopers escorted three people out a door on the far side of the train. They got into waiting SUVs. One vehicle went south on M-24, another headed north on M-24, and the third headed east on I-69. Within minutes the three vehicles had melded into traffic; no one would suspect that the President of the United States might be traveling alongside hundreds of common folk making their way to the beginning of their day.

Within minutes of the incident, Secret Service personnel stormed the building where witnesses claimed the gun was fired. They broke into the room, only to find a high-powered rifle aimed at the podium. Knowing they had a crime scene without a suspect, nothing was touched. CSI was called in to thoroughly scour the room for clues.

Les took out his cell phone and punched in a number.

"I was only able to injure him, and he walked back into the train. I think the majority of people thought he had become ill!" Les said with anger.

"So much for keeping your promise!" Mr. Houchins replied in anger. "Now, listen carefully: do not miss the next time!"

"Yes, sir."

Col. Stocker, his copilot, and reporter Shelly Westbrook roared down the runway and within seconds were airborne and headed for Toronto. Shelly was not searched before takeoff. It was a military flight and security personnel never considered the possibility that a newspaperwoman would be a threat to their pilots or aircraft.

The sky was cloudless, and the farther south they flew, they could see the annual spring-time greening of the land below. It was a great day to fly and Col. Stocker enjoyed the beauty. At this flying altitude, the only metropolitan area he would be able to see would be Minneapolis-St. Paul.

As the Victory Ride continued toward Flint, the national media flashed news bulletins on TV screens all across America.

Brian Williams came on from New York. "We've learned that Leon Abernathy, the Prime Minister of Canada has been shot at an event in Lapeer, Michigan. Mr. Abernathy was with the President and the Governor of Michigan traveling the Grand Trunk Line from Port Huron to New Buffalo. The trio is whistle-stopping across the state of Michigan in celebration of a recently-approved contract for a government high-speed rail system. Let's go to our NBC affiliate WEYI in Saginaw, where correspondent Kim Wiseman has more on this disturbing development."

A solemn dark-haired woman appeared on the screen. "Good morning, Brian. The Prime Minister is alert and appears to have suffered only a minor wound to his upper right arm. Word from inside the train is that, while the wound is more than superficial, there is no fracture and The Prime Minister is expected to make a full and speedy recovery. The more pressing story here is that an assassin in Lapeer attempted to take the Prime Minister's life.

"Shortly after the shooting, a witness saw three cars, driven by state troopers, leave from the back of the train. We expect that these three cars are carrying President Fortner, Governor Halloran, and Prime Minister Abernathy, but that has not been confirmed, Brian."

"Kim, can we assume that the Victory Ride is over and that the three leaders have been escorted out of the area to ensure their safety?"

"That's one assumption, Brian. But the train left Lapeer and there has been no indication that the celebration is over. As I speak, a huge crowd in Flint awaits the arrival of the President and no one has announced that the stop has been cancelled. Obviously, security is on high alert."

Brian Williams reappeared on the screen. "Thank you, Kim. We'll be bringing you more of this developing story. In sum, the Canadian Prime Minister, Leon Abernathy, has been shot in Lapeer, Michigan. He is reported to be fine, suffering no more than a superficial wound to his right arm."

Lou Searing was briefed over the phone by State Police Commander Dick Cellar as he drove to Durand. "Lou, we've had a troubling development."

"Do I turn around and go home?" Lou asked, half in jest.

"No turning around, Lou. We wish you were here already."

"What's going on?" Lou asked.

"The threat has turned real," Dick explained.

"How so?"

"The Prime Minister was wounded in Lapeer. A high-powered rifle was activated across from the train station as Mr. Abernathy began his remarks. The bullet apparently grazed his right arm. The crowd was told he thought he was having a heart attack."

"You said a rifle was activated. Do you mean someone fired the rifle?" Lou asked.

"There was no sign of an assassin. First-responders found an intricate device that would fire the rifle remotely on an electrical signal. So, there is no shooter per se and there are no suspects."

"Did security cameras pick up the person who set it up?" Lou asked.

"They may have. But the device could have been set up before the cameras were in place."

"At any rate, is the Ride over?" Lou asked.

"No, the train and the leaders have moved on."

"No way!" Lou said in disbelief. "You mean to say that a head of state was fired upon, received a wound, and someone advised that the Ride continue? How ludicrous! What kind of advice is the President getting?"

"I know, I know," Col. Cellar said, equally amazed. "The Governor wanted the trip to continue. Festivities are planned in several cities. The President was advised to get off, but he thinks the threat is over now and he feels strongly that the public should be able to see him."

"Oh well, not my call, I guess." Lou realized.

"No, it isn't, but I wanted you to know what happened."

"Thanks. Please tell me that security is on high alert."

"Yes, of course. For the rest of the day, southern Michigan may mirror a police state," Col. Cellar stated.

"I'm just about to Portland, so I'll go right on to Durand. Jack might meet the Ride in Flint. I'm hoping he can get on and learn more."

As Lou approached the I-96 exit for East Lansing, he called Col. Cellar to learn the status of developments.

"The stop in Flint was uneventful, and for that we are most thankful!" Col. Cellar said, relieved.

"All three appeared before the public?" Lou asked.

"Yes. The three vehicles leaving the train in Lapeer were bogus, a ploy to convince anyone associated with the shooting of the Prime Minister that the three VIPs had left the area."

"I see. And nothing suspicious cropped up in Flint?"

"No," Col. Cellar replied. "The Ride is now headed for Durand. We're quite concerned with that stop. Durand is not a stop for the high-speed train, and the town is up in arms. They see themselves as a true railroad town, as they should."

"I think I recall a festival there about trains," Lou said.

"Yes, and they have a museum, and a very nice one at that."

"You think you'll encounter problems?" Lou asked.

"I'm not sure, but it's possible. We hope they only show homemade signs and maybe boo the Governor, and perhaps the President. We hope no one disturbs the festive air by doing something stupid…"

"Like trying to be more successful at killing," Lou said, finishing the thought.

"Exactly."

"Did Jack meet the train in Flint?" Lou asked.

"Yes, he just barely made it."

"Good. We're on the case with Jack there, and I'll join the train in Durand. With luck, the Victory Ride will have only the attempt on the life of the Prime Minister to mar this special day."

"Okay. Lou, I suggest you drive into the downtown area and find Shiawassee County Sheriff Craig Allen. I'll tell him you are about a half-hour away."

"Okay. I don't ask special treatment, but could one of your men pick me up at McDonald's outside of town instead?"

"We'll do that. Call me when you're about five minutes out."

"Will do."

Col. Stocker, his copilot, and Shelly Westbrook were over Minnesota, on course for Wisconsin and then across Lake Michigan. The day continued perfect for a high-altitude flight. Shelly was working on her story on her laptop computer when she received an emergency message from her newspaper. This was usually an alert to a traffic accident, armed robbery, or some other problem in or around Winnipeg. Very rarely did she get news about a Province emergency or trouble in the U.S.A. But high over Minnesota, Shelly opened the site and read, "Prime Minister Abernathy has been shot!"

The news alert continued. "Prime Minister Abernathy was participating in a Victory Ride aboard an Amtrak train in Michigan (U.S.A.) along with U.S. President Fortner and Michigan Governor Roland Halloran. Neither the President nor the Governor was harmed. Prime Minister Abernathy's injury is not life-threatening, but his current location is unknown. The shooter has not been apprehended.

"The security team demanded President Fortner leave the Victory Ride, and it is believed he is in a safe place. On the other hand, Governor Halloran has insisted that the Victory Ride continue. He issued the following statement, "The citizens of Michigan and of the entire United States are shocked that Prime Minister Abernathy was wounded within our borders. He is expected to recover fully, and for this we are thankful. I insist that the Ride continue because of the importance of this project that will bring new jobs to Michigan. The high-speed rail system will enable our State to become a source of expertise for this new and emerging technology. So, we go on to New Buffalo, with sadness for the earlier events of today, but with hope for our future."

While Shelly read of the shooting, Col. Stocker was being briefed by the Canadian Air Force. He was directed to fly to Capital Region International Airport in Lansing, Michigan, to await further orders. He immediately altered course for Lansing.

CHAPTER FIVE

Lou exited I-69 at Durand and pulled into a McDonald's on his right. A police vehicle waited in front of the restaurant. Lou parked in a corner of the lot, and, with his attaché in hand, approached the police car.

"Lou Searing?" the officer asked.

"That's right," Lou replied. "You're my escort to the train station, I presume."

"Yes, sir."

"Anything I should know about?" asked Lou as he entered the vehicle.

"We're on full alert. Stressful, waiting for the other shoe to drop."

Lou could see helicopters and a single-engine plane above Durand. The weather was sunny but chilly. Lou's cell phone rang. "Excuse me, officer."

"Of course."

Lou put the phone to his ear. "Yes."

"Lou, this is Col. Cellar. Just heard something you might find interesting. We've been advised that a Canadian Fighter just received clearance to land in Lansing."

"What's the background on this?" Lou asked.

"A reporter in Winnipeg asked the Canadian Air Force for permission to ride along on the training mission, a scramble to Toronto. Apparently she is writing an article about government readiness in the event of a terrorist attack on a Canadian city."

"I still don't get the significance of what you're telling me," Lou admitted.

"Not sure there is any significance, Lou. It's simply for your information."

"Why will they land in Lansing?" Lou asked.

"It may have something to do with the Victory Ride stop at the Amtrak station in East Lansing."

"Makes sense. Anything else for me?" Lou asked.

"No."

"I'll reach Durand station in a matter of minutes. Will there be a program there—speeches, keys to the city, et cetera?"

"At this point, we are still following protocol, which means bands, speeches, you name it."

"Okay. Jack's on the train. I want to be out with the crowd for now, but I do want to board the Victory Ride on its way to the next stop."

"Not a problem."

Jack Kelly was welcomed onto the Victory Ride in Flint. He and Lou had solved the last five murder investigations in which they had been invited to participate. Most members of the Victory Ride security team were pleased to see him.

"I understand you're having a stressful morning," Jack said to Commander Cellar.

"Puts it mildly, Jack."

"What do I need to know so Lou and I can help?"

"You should probably review all photos, e-mails, briefs, and messages from the FBI, CIA, and the Canadian authorities."

"I will, but first tell me who might have reason to want the Prime Minister killed."

"No person or group has claimed responsibility," Col. Cellar replied. "In fact, we have no calls from witnesses."

"Who are the Prime Minister's enemies?" Jack asked. "Did anyone—an individual or a group—oppose the high-speed rail system? Did influential investors lose money because of the Prime Minister's decision? There was competition for this project in the U.S.—could another state's public be angry because Michigan was chosen?"

"I guess we had better pull in the VIPs to answer some of those questions." He reached for his audio link.

Within a minute the President and Willard Caruthers, his Chief of Staff, appeared in the security car along with the Governor and Jean Arens, his chief administrative assistant."

Col. Cellar introduced Jack to the dignitaries. "This is Jack Kelly, Lou Searing's assistant. He has some questions regarding our circumstances." A sudden increase in the rumbling of the train made it difficult to hear the conversation. Marcia Ludlow wrote on her pad—"Discussion with Lou Searing."

"Thank you." Jack waited for the noise level of the train to die down a bit before continuing, "Did the Prime Minister make enemies in the U.S. or Canada related to this high-speed rail project? Did any one person or group feel they were wrongly rejected?"

Governor Halloran quickly responded, "No question about it. Missouri investors were angry when we got the contract. They wanted to link St. Louis and Kansas City. Others in the Canadian government had planned to put billions into a high-speed rail system from Ottawa to Vancouver. But the decision was made to have a trial run from Toronto to Sarnia and then work with Michigan to have the rail cross Michigan to Chicago. Several provincial governments were not happy!"

Col. Cellar spoke up. "A group of wealthy investors were in favor of the Missouri plan, and when the project was awarded to Michigan and Canada—well, it's hard to describe the political tantrums that took place."

"At this point, U.S. taxpayers are upset with U.S. dollars going to any country other than our own," President Fortner added. "They're thinking nationally, in that all government awards should benefit American workers."

Jack reiterated, "So, there's bad blood between the Missouri contingent and the President. And, you're saying we have not only politicians, but people who lost a lot of money when the project was awarded to Michigan."

"Precisely," the President said, nodding.

"And Ontario and the other provinces wanted the Canadian dollars to build coast-to-coast instead of a hundred-mile section of Ontario," Jack repeated.

"That's right," Col. Cellar replied.

Pierre DeSales, Leon Abernathy's security chief added, "There's another subplot, but I'm not sure it's relevant."

"What's that?" Jack asked.

"In Canada there was a threat on the Prime Minister's life from a media personality. Our security team investigated but found nothing substantial. It might just be something personal, and we couldn't identify a conspiracy."

"So you feel the attempted assassination this morning was directed at the Prime Minister and not the Governor or the President," Jack said, simply looking for agreement.

"That's right," Col. Cellar replied.

"So, can I assume any threat against the Prime Minister would likely come from Canadians?" Jack asked.

"That's right," Pierre said, "because the Prime Minister lobbied for the Toronto and Michigan route. He wanted to work out all the bugs by experimenting on a small stretch. The cost commitment was also a factor, as you can imagine."

"A pilot project costing billions versus one costing trillions?" Jack asked, seeking clarification.

"That's right," Pierre said, nodding.

"Mr. President, what about U.S. competition," Jack asked, with pen in hand. "Were Missouri and Michigan the only states making a pitch?"

"They were two of the main players," the President replied. "Michigan had the veterans in Congress on their side. They also had an edge in train and track manufacturing, and, quite frankly, Michigan had the most to gain in terms of aiding its economy."

"I see. What did Missouri bring to the table?" Jack asked.

"Investors mostly," President Fortner replied. "They had an impressive list."

"There could be a thousand other reasons for the shot this morning," Governor Halloran said. "People with an axe to grind come with political territory, and the attempt on the Prime Minister might have nothing to do with this."

"I agree," Jack said, nodding. "So, what happened in Flint? I arrived after the ceremonies."

Governor Halloran replied, "Flint was a perfect stop. A large and respectful crowd enjoyed seeing the President who charmed them with his knowledge of auto manufacturing and other historical trivia about the Flint area."

"That's good to hear. Let's hope the rest of the day goes just as well."

Jack's cell phone rang. "Excuse me. This is Lou." All nodded as Jack took the call.

"Yes, Lou."

"I take it you are on the Victory Ride?"

"That's correct. I'm talking with the Governor and President and their security teams."

"Well, whoever is behind this now knows you and I are on the case. So keep your wits about you."

"But how could that happen?" Jack asked.

"In today's world, people's movements and communication are easily monitored. Comes with the territory, I guess."

"Is that what you called for?" Jack asked. "Or have you news that might help me?"

"I have a profiler with me at the moment," Lou replied. "I don't mean physically with me, but on an open line. He's a consultant in Chicago."

"Profiler?" Jack asked, not sure he had heard Lou correctly.

"Yes. He specializes in assassination attempts. He's advising me what we might expect as the ride continues."

"What does he think?" Jack asked, curiously.

"He says the most serious concern is the 'I' word."

"The 'I' word?"

"Interruptions," Lou replied firmly. "We should be on guard for a series of interruptions which cause confusion. Interruptions take security's mind off the present, distracting attention from a perpetrator. In fact, the wounding of the Prime Minister might be a distraction for a bigger catastrophe."

"I see."

"And he also advises we watch for unexpected or unusual events," Lou added.

"Like what?" Jack asked.

"A car struck at a crossing, for example, or an emergency alarm, or even a heart attack feigned by someone on board."

"Any of which would divert attention away from the trip running smoothly," Jack replied.

"Correct."

"You may not have heard that at the site of the shooting, security directed the dignitaries to leave the train, and SUVs driven by state troopers were seen leaving the route. In reality, the President and Governor are still on board. It was just a ploy to distract the would-be assassin."

"I'm aware of that," Lou said.

"I assume you want me to keep sniffing around?" Jack asked.

"Yes. Security is very tight here in Durand. Officers from neighboring towns, SWAT teams positioned on top of, or in, buildings, and plain-clothes officers scanning the crowd. People are really coming out for this, school kids especially. For their sakes, I hope nothing happens. We briefed the superintendent of Durand schools, and she is trusting in our security. She wants the kids to have a good memory of Michigan history."

"I understand. I hope it's not a nightmare," Jack responded.

"Stay alert, get as much information as you can, and watch for interruptions."

"Will do."

Having communicated with Jack, Lou turned his attention to the situation in Durand. Obviously this community loved trains, respected their heritage, and enjoyed an association with a traditional America icon, the locomotive. The depot was surrounded by thousands of people who seemed to be enjoying the day and celebrating a new era in rail transportation while honoring the past.

Jack turned back to the dignitaries. "I apologize for that interruption. I think I have enough information. Do you have any questions or information for me?" No one spoke up. "Okay then, thanks for meeting with me."

As they each departed on their separate tasks. Marcia Ludlow approached Jack. "Welcome to the Ride, Lou. We appreciate your assistance." Jack thought it odd that the Head of Homeland Security would not know who he was. He replied, "Jack. My name's Jack Kelly."

"Oh, I'm sorry. I thought you were Mr. Searing." She made note of the interaction on her pad and left.

Jack was beginning to go over the briefing book for the Ride. It contained a huge amount of information about each town along the route, much of it classified.

While Jack studied a document from the CIA, he was approached by Betty Willoughby, Marcia Ludlow's assistant. "Excuse me, Mr. Kelly. Who authorized you to board this train?"

"I'm not sure. Lou Searing told me to join the train in Flint. There was no question when I said who I was."

"So, whoever let you board did not ask for identification or anything official allowing you access to this train?"

"No."

"Who let you board?" Betty asked.

"I don't know. A man in a suit. He was pleasant, cordial, and helpful."

"I see."

"I take it there is a problem with my being here?" Jack asked.

"There certainly is. You are not authorized to be here and you've had access to the President, Governor, their traveling delegation, and security officers. We'll need to isolate you for the remainder of this ride."

"I don't think you understand: Mr. Searing and I have been asked to assist all of you."

"Correction: Mr. Searing was asked. For all we know, you could be the assassin!"

"Well, I'm not. I need to call Lou."

"No, you won't be calling or seeing anyone. You are in a sense quarantined for the remainder of this trip, or until your presence is authorized."

"Not to appear rude, Miss Willoughby, but when the Governor asked Lou to become involved, I was included."

"Did the Governor specifically invite you to participate?" Betty asked.

"I have no idea," Jack replied. "But Lou and I always work as a team."

"In this instance, every person must be individually cleared to participate."

"Then why did you allow me on the train?" Jack asked, bristling at the lack of respect.

"By mistake," Betty answered. "Whoever allowed you to board obviously thought you were Mr. Searing. And now we can't allow you to leave the train or talk to anyone outside because you have information that could jeopardize the trip."

"I presume you will call Mr. Searing and explain this to him?" Jack asked.

"Yes. We will handle that."

This is not going to be pretty, Jack thought.

"Mr. Searing? Capital Security Agent, Tomas McBride calling."

"Yes?"

"We have a Jack Kelly on the Victory Ride train. Office of Homeland Security representatives on the train thought you were boarding and later they discovered that the man is not you, but Mr. Kelly."

"That's right. He's my associate. We work together."

"But there was no security check done on him," replied Mr. McBride.

"There doesn't need to be," Lou replied harshly. "I agreed to help the Governor under the assumption that Mr. Kelly would assist me. The Governor knows we work together, and quite frankly, that's why he asked me to get involved."

"I'm sorry, Mr. Searing, but this is a serious breach of protocol. Mr. Kelly has seen our set-up on this train and talked with people on the train, so we can't release him; he must stay on the train."

"Don't be ridiculous," Lou said, beginning to get angry. "Put the Governor on."

"I'm afraid that's not possible. He's talking with the President concerning events in Durand."

Lou mentally counted to ten. "OK. When you get a chance to talk to the Governor, please explain this conversation to him. And then tell him that Mr. Searing has rescinded his agreement to assist in his safety."

Lou's displeasure was turning into anger. "And when the train gets to Durand, either you let me on board or you let Mr. Kelly off. If you do neither, I will personally see to it that not only are you removed from your duty, but your office will be embarrassed, and if it's possible, you'll be guests of honor on *60 Minutes*. Do you understand?"

"I know you're angry, but our protocol demands I take this action."

"I understand, but my protocol demands the action I take.

"I'm sure the Governor will contact you, Mr. Searing."

Lou pushed the 'END' key.

The Governor's security agent returned to Betty and Jack. "Your friend, Mr. Searing, is not a happy man."

Why am I not surprised? Jack asked himself with a slight smile. "Trust me; Lou is a mild-mannered man. You can count on one hand the number of people who have seen him angry. But when someone takes control of the people who work with him without his consent, it's not pretty."

"He's simply a citizen," Betty remarked. "He's not nearly as important as he seems to think he is."

"Okay," Jack replied shaking his head in amazement at this slip in courtesy. "Sit back and enjoy the show."

"He demands that Mr. Kelly be let off the train in Durand," Agent McBride said to Betty.

Jack said nodding, "Sounds like him. I think your word choice, 'demands' is correct."

"Meaning?" McBride asked, quizzically.

"Meaning you had better open the door in Durand and either let him in or let me off."

"I can't do that!" Betty exclaimed. "You've seen and heard highly-classified information!"

"I'll be ready to leave," Jack said calmly. "You simply tell me when to get off the train."

"You will not get off this train, Mr. Kelly!" Betty was red-faced with anger. Jack shook his head, still smiling.

Lou was beside himself; he had never encountered anyone who summarily mistrusted his judgment. You simply didn't ask Lou Searing to work on a case and then put up a barrier to his investigation. He made a mental note to check his emotions at the car door and not rant to the sheriff.

Head of security operations in Durand was the Shiawassee County Sheriff, Craig Allen. Noticing the wide array of law enforcement officers, Craig turned to the Durand Chief of Police, Tim Hall, and said, "Keep your fingers crossed. Any thief who wants to rob a bank today will have no fear of us. This is a robber's day if ever there was one."

"I don't think you need to worry, Sheriff," Chief Hall replied. "Everyone in the county will be here for this historic occasion. In fact, I think the bank presidents may have taken your advice and closed for a block of time during the Victory Ride's visit."

"Guess you're right."

"Who is this guy coming toward us?" Tim asked.

"Lou Searing," Sheriff Allen remarked. "You are about to be in the presence of greatness."

"Really?"

"This man has solved every crime he's been asked to look into."

"Sort of a modern day 'Colombo?'" Tim asked.

"You might say that."

"Where's the cigar, trench coat, and Basset hound?" Tim asked with a chuckle.

"The guy hasn't any trademarks. He just gets his head into a problem and doesn't come up for air until it's solved."

"What's he doing here in Durand?"

"Governor's office wanted him involved."

"Involved in what?" Tim asked. "A crime in Durand?"

"Not as far as I know, and you'd be the second to know."

"So, he's good, huh?" Chief Hall asked.

"You might have a chance to see for yourself. Last year the Sheriff's Association named him Man of the Year. It is the first time they didn't honor one of their own since the Association began decades ago."

With hand out-stretched, Lou approached the two men. "Good morning, Sheriff Allen." The sheriff returned Lou's firm handshake.

"So far, yes, it's a good morning," Craig replied. "Great to see you, Lou, but your presence may be a bad omen."

"Let's hope this Victory Ride pulls out of Durand as safe and secure as it pulls in," Lou remarked enthusiastically.

"I say, 'Amen' to that."

Lou saw people all around, even children perched in trees, and every store and apartment window occupied with stretched necks. Everyone hoped to get a glimpse of the President and Governor on this historic day.

Just as Lou was about to ask a series of questions a radio squawked. The sheriff said, "Excuse me, Lou."

A deputy on the outskirts of town was reporting. "There's been an accident on I-69. Traffic is backing up. I need some help out here."

"Okay, it's coming. Is the backup westbound or eastbound?" Sheriff Allen asked.

"Both. A semi jackknifed heading eastbound. Several cars swerved and crossed the median, striking westbound vehicles. It's a mess. It'll be closed for several hours."

"Are the State Police on the scene?"

"They're en route."

"Good, I can't release anyone from this area. We'll need to alert EMS crews of Alternate Route B if they need to get to a hospital."

"Right. Entrance ramps onto 69 will be closed."

"Roger. When you're rerouting traffic, don't send them into Durand."

"Try not to, Sheriff."

"One thing after another, I take it," Lou said, as the word 'Interruptions' flashed into his mind.

"Multiple-vehicle accident out on 69. I told the Governor's people when they planned this that there might be problems. But, no, the Governor wanted to celebrate this coup with the President and the legislators. This isn't about a speed-rail system coming to Michigan, this is about the Governor becoming Secretary of Transportation or Commerce or something in Washington."

"You're probably right, but we're here, Sheriff. Any threats you're aware of?" Lou asked.

"Nope, been quiet."

"I'm going to board the Victory Ride when it pulls out of town. In the meantime, I have work to do."

"Let me know if you need anything," Sheriff Allen said.

"I appreciate that," Lou replied.

Lou called Col. Cellar. "What can you tell me about the accident on 69?"

"It's a multiple-vehicle pileup. Chain reaction after a truck jackknifed near the 118 mile marker on eastbound 69."

"What company did the semi belong to?" Lou asked.

"Not sure at this point, but it's a Canadian Company."

"A lot of trucks go to Canada along 69," Lou said, realizing Interstate 69 goes directly into Canada.

"And those truckers are not happy."

"High-speed rail will be a competitor, I take it," Lou replied.

"You got that right. Truckers in Canada and the United States lobbied heavily and spent millions of dollars to derail— pun intended—this project."

"I see," Lou replied. "Goods can be shipped in less time using high-speed rail than by trucks—cheaper too."

"Exactly."

"Do you think they're behind the threat?" Lou asked.

"If they aren't, my deductive reasoning skills are deader than a door knob."

"Okay, keep me in the loop about this accident."

"I'll be in touch when I know something."

Lou checked his watch and saw 11:15 a.m. The Durand High School band was playing *God Bless America,* and the crowd was singing loudly. The cheerleaders were getting people excited about the soon-to-arrive dignitaries. Children and adults carried signs made of cardboard and poster board reading, "MI, U.S.A., and Ontario; Friends for Progress!" "Thanks, Mr. President!" "Our Governor is Bringing JOBS to Michigan!" Many people were wearing round commemorative pins with colorful words: 'A Victory Ride for Michiganians.' The pins were sold for a dollar in each city by the Chamber of Commerce. April 25 was destined to go down in the history books as one of the most important days for the State of Michigan.

CHAPTER SIX

While the anticipation of seeing the dignitaries grew in Durand, four men from Missouri were en route to Kalamazoo. Their 2011 BMW sedan sped along U.S. 57 toward Chicago and then east to I-94 and to their destination, Kalamazoo.

As Lou approached downtown Durand, he began to settle down. His heart rate slowed, and his blood pressure returned to normal. As he walked through the crowd, he heard train whistles approaching from the east. The middle school band played *Michigan My Michigan, O Canada,* and then joined the high school band to play the *Star Spangled Banner.* The train came into view about a quarter-mile from the station, slowly approaching the makeshift podium where the speakers would stand behind a bullet-proof shield.

After a good ten minutes, Dale Joan Carlson, the mayor of Durand, approached the microphone. "Mr. President, Mr. Prime Minister, and Governor Halloran, the citizens of Durand, a community proud of its railroad heritage, welcome you to our city. We pledge to work with you in building the prototype speed-rail system through our area. This technology will put Durand on the map. Our community is known for the Michigan Railroad History Museum, and today I pledge that we will also build a museum dedicated to high-speed rail. Even though our town will not be a stop, people will come to Durand to visit the world's only High-Speed Rail Museum. In fact, photos taken today will be displayed in this state-of-the-art building." The crowd cheered.

"And now, it is my honor to give you the Governor of Michigan, the Honorable Roland Halloran."

Everyone cheered and waved amidst shouts of, "Welcome, Mr. Governor!"

Standing safely behind the bullet-proof glass, the Governor began, "Thank you, Mrs. Carlson, and thank you my fellow Michiganians. I am pleased to hear about your museum. Wow! This is a surprise and wonderful news!

"I am honored to present to you the Prime Minister of Canada, the Honorable Leon Abernathy." As the Prime Minister walked to the podium, the Governor stepped to his left beyond the protective shield. He stood still and erect as the Prime Minister placed his notes on the podium. School children waved Canadian flags in honor of the Canadian leader.

The Prime Minister began. "Your neighbors to the east and north welcome our working together to bring high-speed transportation to our respective countries. After the completion of this short-distance cooperative effort, we hope to build a trans-continental high-speed rail system across all seven of Canada's provinces.

"This effort would not have been possible without a shared vision. The credit, of course, goes to your President and my good friend, Alan Fortner." The crowd erupted into applause and cheers.

"It is now my pleasure to present your President, the Honorable Alan Fortner."

The Durand High School Band played *Hail to the Chief* as the President came out of the train and took his place behind the bullet-proof shield. The Prime Minister immediately went into the train, avoiding any further exposure.

An array of photographers snapped hundreds of photos, for this was the first and undoubtedly only time that a sitting governor, the Prime Minister of Canada, and the President of the United States had visited Durand together.

The President waved to the crowd. After a thirty-second pause to allow for photographs, the President resumed his stance behind the microphone. "My fellow Americans. The people of Durand appreciate history and the people who make history. Railroads have been a mainstay in the transportation of goods and people since the early days of our country. We are now about to embark on a new chapter in the life of the railroad, and I am pleased to hear that this city will incorporate that chapter into the new proposed museum. In fact, I promise you today that I will attend your ribbon-cutting ceremony, either as your

President, or former President." Once again the crowd cheered enthusiastically.

The President particularly enjoyed his popularity in Durand. He went on a bit longer offering comments reflecting his agenda for the country. He ended with praise for standing firm in the recession and believing in America. He waved again, then entered the train to continue westward.

Lou had every intention of following through on his threat: if Jack Kelly couldn't get off the train, there would be a price to pay. Looking up and down the train for any indication that Jack was outside, he became convinced that Jack was not going to appear.

Lou reached into the breast pocket of his jacket and retrieved an FBI badge, an honor arranged for by Michigan's Attorney General in the previous administration, after Lou had solved his tenth murder case. Lou had read the paperwork that came with the honor more than once, and he knew the badge was more than an item to display in a trophy case.

The badge gave him access to certain FBI facilities in the United States, and to any non-classified information he wanted; he could also become involved in any crime or potential crime against the federal government. Since the President of the United States and other federal officials were on the Victory Ride, he could, if he wished, board the train for whatever purpose he deemed important.

The ceremony over, citizens returned home, to school, or to their places of work, as a construction crew moved the platform back from the train. Lou interrupted the workers. "Excuse me. I want to board the train, and I'm authorized to do so."

"Not my call," said one of the workers. "I'm pretty sure it's locked up, but rap on the door, and someone might hear you."

Lou did as suggested. An armed security officer appeared and opened the door a few inches. "This train is off-limits. Please leave."

Lou calmly reached into his breast pocket, retrieved the badge in its leather case, and flashed it to the security officer. The officer glanced at it and replied, "I'm sorry, Mr. Searing. Come in."

"Thank you. I wish to speak to Agent McBride."

"One moment, sir."

The security officer locked the door behind Lou and offered him a seat in the security car. After about five minutes, Agent McBride appeared. "Mr. Searing, I presume."

"Correct. I've come to take Mr. Kelly off the train."

"I explained this to you when we talked on the phone. Mr. Kelly is not permitted to leave because he has seen and read classified information and has not undergone a security check."

Lou countered, "And I explained to you that we are a team, and when he's working with me, he has the same clearances I have."

"Obviously we're not on the same page," Agent McBride replied.

Lou said with an equally strong voice, "I know protocol, and I follow it. Remember, I gave you the option of settling this with your director first."

Agent McBride spoke stiffly. "I don't need to call the director. I'm following protocol of the Bureau, and I won't bother him with a minor issue."

"Either you call the director, or I will," Lou protested. "I want this resolved—soon."

Lou took his phone from his pocket and punched in the number that would connect him to Robert Singleton, the Director of the Federal Bureau of Investigation.

"Good morning, Robert. This is Lou Searing."

"Good morning, Lou. Good to hear from you."

"Thank you, Chief. I'm sorry to bother you with this, but Security Agent McBride on the Victory Ride refuses to…"

"I know all about it, Lou. I was about to call Agent McBride and report that a security check has been done on Mr. Kelly. He can resume his work with you on the Victory Ride."

"Thank you, but Agent McBride needs to understand that when I'm invited to work a case, so is Jack. He works with me, and is to be accorded respect."

"Absolutely, Lou. Apparently I didn't communicate well enough with our security personnel. It's a complicated threat, and we need you. I know a happy Lou Searing is more effective than an unhappy one, so please accept my apology."

"Apology accepted, Chief. Thank you. Good-bye."

The Victory Ride pulled away from Durand carrying Lou and Jack on the train. Lou would make arrangements to get his car later. For the moment, he was right where he wanted to be.

CHAPTER SEVEN

As Col. Stocker landed at the Capital Region International Airport in Lansing, he apologized to his passenger. "Sorry about this. You never know when plans will change. Who knows? You might find something interesting to add to your story."

"I don't have my passport with me," Shelly said, illegally standing on foreign soil.

"That's not a problem. You're with me, and in that respect, you're part of the Canadian Air Force. Besides, I'm fairly sure you won't be asked for it anyway. I could be ordered back into the sky at any moment."

"Or, we could be here for a day or two?" Shelly asked.

"Unless there's an international crisis, I expect I'll be ordered back to Winnipeg. We just need to be patient."

"Am I free to go into Lansing?" Shelly asked.

"I don't see any reason why not. As long as I can reach you by cell and you're here within a half-hour of my ordered departure, there should be no problem. Just don't get into any trouble, or your lack of passport could be a problem."

"I'd like to go to the Lansing State Journal to check the wire for late news. And I can make contacts there, should I need help for a future story."

Shelly took a cab to the Lansing State Journal on Lenawee Street. The cab driver accepted Shelly's Canadian currency. As a visiting journalist, she was directed to the office of the editor, Tina Block.

Tina greeted her warmly. "Welcome. It's rare that we have an award-winning Canadian journalist in our midst."

"The visit is a surprise to me, too," Shelly said. "I'm doing a story about the readiness of our Air Force to respond to an international terrorist attack in, say, Toronto."

"That could be a Pulitzer Prize waiting for you," Tina said with a smile.

"I doubt it. It's a fairly dull topic and story-line."

"Unless, of course, you happen upon some sort of major event," Tina replied.

"Highly unlikely, but yes, I see your point."

"Well, as fate would have it, we're facing a possible crisis next door in East Lansing. I assume you're aware of the Victory Ride taking place today across Michigan?"

"I haven't heard about it," Shelly admitted. "What's being celebrated? Something about sports, I suppose."

"Actually, no. Canada and the United States are going to work together to create an international high-speed rail system from Toronto to Chicago."

"Oh, I know about that. I'm not sure it should be called 'Victory' but I know what you mean."

"You did hear that your Prime Minister was shot when the train stopped in Lapeer?" Tina asked.

"Yes. I suspect that is why we were ordered to land here?" Shelly replied.

"The wire story says he sustained only a superficial wound. It doesn't say whether he was hospitalized," Tina said, holding a copy of the Associated Press story.

"Excuse me—I must call my editor."

Shelly's call went right through. "Hello, Shelly. How is your trip going?" Susan asked.

"Well, I'm in Lansing, Michigan, at the moment."

"Why?" Susan asked.

"Col. Stocker was directed to land here and await orders. He didn't tell me why, nor would I expect him to."

"Well, we're tracking that so-called Victory Ride because of the Prime Minister. Let me take a look at our update. Yes, the train is passing through Perry, Michigan, due in East Lansing in eleven minutes."

"I'm going to the station in East Lansing. I'll call you later." Shelly hung up abruptly.

Col. Stocker sat in the waiting room of the General Aviation Terminal near the Capital Region International Airport reading *Aviation Today* when he received a call. "Colonel, you're to continue to Toronto and complete your mission. A crisis in Michigan didn't materialize. Follow Ground Control directions as you leave for Toronto."

"Roger. Request 30 minutes of preparation time."

"Roger. Granted."

When Col. Stocker called Shelly there was no answer, so he left a message, "I've orders to leave immediately, so return to the airport ASAP. Departure at 1230 hours."

The State Journal had provided a driver and vehicle to take Shelly to the Amtrak station in East Lansing. She had turned off her cell phone in the Lansing State Journal office and tucked it into her travel bag. When she left, her mind was on one thing: getting to the Amtrak station for the Victory Ride's arrival. She missed Col. Stocker's call—plain and simple.

Once the security personnel realized that Lou and Jack were on their side, they treated the two as consultants.

"I'm sorry I wasted time and energy with protocol," Betty Willoughby apologized.

"We understand," Lou replied, trying to let the snub pass.

"Let's just get on with this case," Jack said.

Lou asked, "My first question is why this 'Victory Ride' is still going forward? After an attempt on the Prime Minister's life, I would expect you to shut down the train and get the VIPs to a safe place. You're crazy to keep them in a capsule without a way to maneuver. They're sitting ducks!"

"They insisted that the ride continue," Betty explained. "They call the shots, and we do what we can to protect them."

"But certainly as security people you agree they're making a huge mistake?"

"Of course, of course," Betty agreed.

"I'd like to speak to them," Lou said.

"They're in the security car. We can go talk to them."

"All in the same car?" Lou asked, astonished. "I don't believe it. Is this information public?"

"We didn't broadcast it, if that's what you mean, but I suppose someone could figure it out," Betty explained.

"This is not good at all," Lou said shaking his head. "Governor Halloran mentioned to me that this trip offered national leaders the chance to converse. And he can inform the President and the Prime Minister about Michigan issues. But all staying in the same car..."

"On Mackinac Island maybe, but not on a train moving through open country. It might as well be open season on politicians," Jack replied.

"Let's go." Lou, Jack, and Betty moved into the security car. Introductions were made, and Governor Halloran explained why Lou and Jack were on board.

"Mr. President, these are two of Michigan's finest detectives. When I received the threatening call, I asked Lou to become involved. We're fortunate to have them on the Victory Ride."

"Thank you, Governor Halloran, but let's not waste time with pleasantries," Lou replied. "We've got work to do, and we want to talk to the three of you to see what can be learned. In the first place, I don't understand your decision to continue, in light of the threat on your lives and your wounding, sir." Lou nodded toward Leon.

"Lou, we can't lose touch with the people," the Governor replied. "We receive threats every day—you'd be amazed how often."

"That's fair, but you three are sitting ducks here in one car on a train in farm country!"

"But this is a huge celebration for Michigan and Canada!" the Governor said eagerly. "In fact, this high-speed rail system may very well save this State—it's as simple as that. The number of potential jobs and the opportunity to lead the U.S. in future transportation are, as I said, huge!"

"I understand, but you three don't need to risk your lives to celebrate," Lou advised.

"Perhaps we do," the Governor continued. "The people need to see their President, who made this possible. He and his staff worked behind the scenes to secure the votes for Michigan to be awarded the contract."

"But the risk to your safety..." Lou interrupted.

"People are lined up along this route. Thousands at each stop, with school bands, local dignitaries, and the media. We were on the *Today Show* this morning. We'll be on all three networks at 6:00 p.m. Simply put, Michigan may be reborn this day, and I refuse to give in to a threat. Obviously I am appalled that the Prime Minister was shot on Michigan soil, but the wound was superficial, and he has bravely agreed to keep the activities on schedule."

Lou sighed in resignation. "Tell us all you know about the threat and the shooting," Lou asked.

"The threat came in a phone call to my office," the Governor began. "The caller said that the Victory Ride was doomed, and that enemies of Michigan and Ontario would be using life-threatening tactics."

"Was the call traced?" Jack asked.

"Yes. It was from a cell phone in Canada."

"Has the shooter been identified?" Lou asked.

"No. Witnesses saw someone suspicious leaving a building near the Amtrak station, but we lost him in the crowd. We have viewed video from the train scanning the crowd, but nobody else seemed suspicious."

"So, you don't know if other action is planned?" Jack asked.

"Precisely. That's why we chose to go ahead with the ceremonies in other communities. The shooter took one shot, missed, thankfully, and the fear is over as far as the Victory Ride is concerned. Of course, law enforcement in Michigan and Canada will investigate this assassination attempt and find whoever fired the shot or those who were behind it."

"We're about to stop in East Lansing," Lou stated, taking a deep breath. "We proceed as originally planned?"

"Correct. We've had successful stops in Flint and Durand. I am assuming that security will be tightened. There will be more plainclothes officers in the crowd, and we'll add a SWAT team that was originally on stand-by. But, whoever fired the shot would be insane to attempt another, that is, unless he or she is on a suicide mission."

"I understand, but anyone who physically threatens the life of another is insane, whether at the first attempt or a second," Lou said, shaking his head.

The Missouri car had entered Michigan on I-94. Fortunately, or unfortunately, a Michigan State Trooper pulled over the vehicle near the New Buffalo exit.

"You folks from Missouri are in an awful big hurry today," Trooper Jose Gomez remarked as he approached the driver's side of the vehicle.

"Yes, Officer. I guess we are. I apologize."

"May I see your license, registration, and proof of insurance please?"

As the driver offered his license, the front-seat passenger interrupted. "Trooper, I am the Governor of Missouri. We were going over the speed limit, and for that I'm sorry, but I'm sure you realize we have immunity."

"Immunity from what?" Trooper Gomez asked; he had never pulled over a governor from another state.

"Immunity from prosecution for violating laws in another state."

"News to me," Jose replied. "Sit tight. I'll be back."

Trooper Gomez entered his cruiser and picked up his radio while cars seemed to fly by in the far left lane. He called base. The dispatcher acknowledged his call.

"I've pulled over a car with Missouri plates. One of the passengers claims to be the Governor of Missouri; he says he's immune from prosecution."

"Generally that's correct. How fast did you clock him?"

"Eighty-five."

"Was he driving in a reckless manner?"

"No, just flying low."

"Did the driver have a Missouri Government ID?"

"I didn't ask for it. He gave me a Missouri license issued in Jefferson City, Missouri. He has no history of moving violations."

"I'll take responsibility for this," the dispatcher replied. "Let him go, but ask him to obey the speed laws in Michigan. Another stop will net him a less warm second greeting."

"Copy that."

Fifteen minutes after Col. Stocker called Shelly, she made her way with camera and notepad in hand into the space reserved for the media outside the East Lansing Amtrak station. This was as close as people were allowed to the podium.

The crowd was a mixture of Michigan State University students, school children, and adults from East Lansing and surrounding communities. The MSU marching band entertained the crowd with patriotic songs. They occasionally played the Spartan Fight Song, and Sparty, the university mascot, mingled with the crowd. It was a celebration almost equal to the Spartan basketball team returning victorious from an NCAA tourney.

Col. Stocker called his commander at the Winnipeg base. "I'm ready to leave, but the passenger authorized to fly with me is not here."

"You let her leave?"

"Yes, sir. She wanted to go to the local newspaper office and had a cell phone. I've tried to reach her, but she doesn't respond."

"Weren't you warned not to let her out of your sight? Isn't that standard operating procedure?"

"Yes, sir. She was authorized to fly the scramble with me, but we weren't meant to land. I was to fly to Toronto, rendezvous with other aircraft from eastern cities, and then return to base."

"You need to continue the mission immediately. I'll worry about getting the reporter back to Winnipeg."

"Yes, sir."

Les Trousard's route to East Lansing took him through several small mid-Michigan communities, so he was careful to observe traffic laws. Along Haslett Road he came upon a police seatbelt check-lane. He tugged at his belt, making sure it was buckled.

As he cautiously drove through the check point, a police car with swirling red and blue lights pulled behind his vehicle. Les immediately pulled over. Again he checked his belt and found it to be secure. Les told his passenger to make sure his belt was locked. He could only imagine that somehow he had been spotted leaving Lapeer.

"You drove without a seatbelt through the check point, sir." An officer from the Meridian Township Police said, standing close to the driver's window.

"That's not true, Officer," Les countered. "My belt was locked. Someone is mistaken."

"Please give me your license, registration, and proof of insurance."

The officer stepped away from Les's car. Les glanced at his watch—he was now three minutes behind schedule for completing his mission.

The Meridian Township Officer moved slowly back to Les's car. "I think I know what happened. Your jacket and your seatbelt are both black. I believe your belt was locked, and I think the officer failed to notice the matching colors. You're free to go. I apologize for interrupting your day. Please continue to use your seatbelt and drive safely."

"Thank you," sighed Les. He pulled away with a fast-beating heart, checking his GPS. It would guide him to the Amtrak station, where he would continue his mission. He had missed killing the Prime Minister in Lapeer, but he intended to be successful in East Lansing.

Most attention was focused on the north side of the train in East Lansing, where the three government leaders would stand. The south side of the train was overseen by a single East Lansing police officer carrying a rifle, who walked the length of the multi-car train.

The noise on the north side was on occasion deafening, with bands playing, the crowd cheering, and long interludes of applause. The guard behind the train didn't hear footsteps, nor did he know a Taser had hit him. He lay next to the rails on the roadbed, paralyzed. The man with the Taser stripped the officer and took his rifle. Les donned the uniform over his light slacks and shirt. He put the rifle over his shoulder and joined the crowd. He was simply one more security officer.

On the north side of the train, the people attending the Victory Ride enjoyed the pomp and circumstance. The mayors of East Lansing and Lansing gave short welcoming speeches, praising Governor Halloran and the President for bringing this economic opportunity to Michigan.

The Governor repeated his words from the Flint and Durand stops. He introduced President Fortner who sounded like a proud alumnus of Michigan State University. He congratulated the administration for effective leadership at one of the first land grant institutions. He told the crowd he was cheering for the Spartans in the NCAA Tourney and that if the stop could be extended he would go over to the Breslin Center and take on the Green and White in a friendly scrimmage.

The President introduced Canada's Prime Minister, but the Prime Minister did not get off the train. A few uncomfortable seconds passed before an aide to the Prime Minister approached the President and whispered into his ear, "The Prime Minister received a call from his office in Ottawa. He is talking with his secretary. Apparently there has been some tragedy in Vancouver. He apologizes, but will not be able to address the crowd."

The President approached the microphone and addressed the waiting crowd, "The Prime Minister sends his greetings. He has an emergency to deal with in the western part of Canada and won't be offering remarks. I can tell you that if he could step out here he would offer his congratulations to Michigan for being awarded the high-speed rail contract and he would pledge to work with us in the future."

The President turned to the Governor, who signaled that he wished to speak. The President said his farewell to the mid-Michigan crowd, waved to all, and entered the train.

While speaking on the phone, the Prime Minister looked out at the crowd—specifically those in the media section. Shelly Westbrook was the last person he had expected to see in Michigan. She had been a leading political reporter in Ottawa, and it was through his action that she had been reassigned to Winnipeg.

When the Prime Minister finished his talk, he called for Pierre, his security chief.

"I saw Shelly Westbrook in the media section. I want her arrested immediately!"

"Yes, sir."

Les was beside himself. He could not fulfill his mission. The Prime Minister was never off the train, but Les knew that he would be blamed for the failed attempt. Mr. Houchins would be furious. But there were other stops to come. Les knew he would be successful. He'd just have to figure out how to execute the assassination.

During the closing remarks by Governor Halloran, a member of the Canadian Security detail approached Shelly, took her by the arm, and calmly told her she was under arrest. Shelly sighed and moved away with the security guard. Once they were away from the crowd, the guard suddenly fell forward. To an onlooker, it appeared he had fainted. There was no gunshot, no other sound when the man was hit. Randall Beaver had been watching Shelly and when he saw that she was in trouble, he quickly took out the officer.

Shelly got the attention of people around her and asked that they call 911. As more people began to gather, sirens sounded in the distance. Shelly quickly picked up her travel bag and purse and walked away. All of the crowd's attention was on the man lying face down on the pavement. Although Shelly managed to slip away, she was known to Prime Minister Abernathy and to law enforcement.

During the East Lansing celebration, Lou and Jack remained on the train, observing the goings on through the media car window. They didn't see or hear anything out of the ordinary. But news of the Tasering of the East Lansing police officer and the attack on the Canadian Security Guard quickly spread throughout the Victory Ride and those in the crowd who stayed after the ceremony.

"Conspiracy," Lou said.

"Yup," Jack replied. "It seems obvious, so I suppose neither of us gets any points as seers."

"Dare I say it's a Canadian conspiracy?" Lou asked.

"Well, the Canadian Prime Minister was wounded, and a Canadian security officer was incapacitated while arresting a Canadian reporter, so it appears that way," Jack added.

"The Victory Ride should end here in East Lansing," Lou said firmly. "This has gone far enough."

Lou asked to speak with the three leaders. "Had enough?" Lou asked.

"I've had enough, yes," the Prime Minister nodded. "I could handle the wound, but an attack on one of my security officers is enough for me to leave. You can carry on, but for me, I must get back to Ottawa to figure out what's going on."

"We understand, and will cooperate one hundred percent in your investigation of these crimes," Governor Halloran replied.

Leon Abernathy walked solemnly to his compartment. He contacted Pierre and directed that he return to Ottawa. Pierre immediately put Leon's departure plan in motion.

Shelly realized that her cell phone's battery was dead in her travel bag when she was arrested and that she was now stranded in Lansing, Michigan, without a passport. She had little money which was in Canadian currency. She managed to get back to the quickly-dispersing crowd, and found her escort from the State Journal. She asked to be taken to General Aviation, in hopes of connecting with Col. Stocker for a ride home.

CHAPTER EIGHT

First Lieutenant Lawrence Williams, commander of the St. Joseph Michigan State Police Post, called Lansing headquarters.

"Something's come up that I want you to know about," Commander Williams began.

"Go ahead," an Operations Lieutenant replied.

"One of my troopers stopped a Missouri-registered vehicle going 85 near New Buffalo."

"Okay. Why do I need to know about it?"

"A passenger in the vehicle was the Governor of Missouri who claimed he had immunity. Can governors go as fast as they want in each other's states?"

"I wouldn't say, 'as fast as they want,' but it's an accepted practice. Governors don't like to embarrass one another."

"I understand. I just thought I'd pass along the information," Lt. Williams said.

"I'll let Governor Halloran know. Our daily briefing doesn't show any governor visiting Michigan today. We usually get a protection assignment when a sitting governor visits the state."

"Sorry to bother you with the routine," Lawrence said apologetically.

"No problem. It could be important in a way we don't know at the moment."

Lt. Williams decided to call Col. Cellar to inform him the Missouri Governor's presence in Michigan. Col. Cellar turned to Governor Halloran.

"Were you expecting a visit from the Governor of Missouri today?"

"No. It's protocol for one governor to let another know when he or she is planning to visit. Governor Wright knows protocol and expects it in Missouri, so I am surprised he would be in Michigan without my knowledge. Where was he going?"

"I don't know. He was eastbound on I-94 and was pulled over near New Buffalo."

"Was he ticketed?"

"No, he said he had immunity."

"There's no such thing!" Governor Halloran exclaimed. "A governor has to follow the laws of any state just like any other citizen!"

"Our trooper checked with the post commander, and since reckless driving wasn't involved, the driver got a warning."

"I'll have to remember that the next time I'm going through Missouri."

"Does this concern you, Governor?" Col. Cellar asked.

"The last interaction I had with Wright was quite hostile," Governor Halloran recalled.

"What was the issue?"

"This high-speed rail contract. Missouri interests spent a lot of money lobbying for it and Wright thought they had it locked up. He was really upset when we got the contract. He blamed the President for lobbying on our behalf, and he blamed the Prime Minister for convincing the President that it was better to start with a short route between the U.S.A. and Canada. I doubt I've ever seen another head of state so angry at losing a project. Most of us fight, and if we lose, we lose. We lick our wounds, get up, and try again. But, Governor Wright put all of his eggs into one basket, solicited a lot of wealthy people, and convinced them to put millions into a lobbying effort. He likely promised a huge return on their investments. When Michigan got the contract, he had to face all those entrepreneurs and admit failure."

"Do you think he'd come after you, Governor?" Col. Cellar asked bluntly.

"Meaning kill me?" Roland asked.

"Well, yes, I guess so."

"That would be political suicide. He wants to become a Senator or even Vice President. Killing me would end those hopes. He's an angry man, but not a stupid man. No, I don't think he is coming to kill me."

"What is he doing in Michigan then?"

"I have no idea."

While arrangements were being made for the Prime Minister and his entourage to leave the train secretly, Lou and Jack asked more questions.

"Who is the reporter you spotted in the media section?" Lou asked Leon.

"Shelly Westbrook," Leon grimaced. "She was a reporter in Ottawa, and a good one. But, with the referendum on French becoming Canada's official language, she seemed to change from a solid reporter to a radical, biased, ax-to-grind activist. She stirred people up and led them in demonstrations. It was scary because people seemed to do whatever she asked. After the referendum, she took on another cause: immigration. Your Mexicans are our Americans. She led a strong nationalistic effort, even though I'm sure most Canadians welcome American citizens. She became unreasonable and destructive of attempts to bring our citizens together and to compromise."

"So, you were instrumental in having her sent to Winnipeg, her private Siberia," Jack said, noting Shelly's transfer.

"Most certainly. She was a Canadian citizen, and the only way I could try to limit her compulsive activism was to see if I could 'deport' her, so to speak."

"So, you contacted the editor of the Ottawa Gazette?" Lou said.

"That's right; I invited the editor to my office, and we talked. He understood my position, but he seemed to like her style and the way she motivated the public."

"I imagine it sells papers," Jack added.

"Yes, it does, and even though I didn't much appreciate her, thousands did. The editor finally agreed to what I asked, and assigned her thousands of miles from the capital of Canada."

"Why didn't she simply quit her job and stay in Ottawa to lead her flock of activists?" Jack asked, pen ready for Leon's response.

"She needed the job and the forum to promote her ideas. I'm not certain, but I sense that she and the paper agreed to some terms."

Lou got right to the point. "Could she be the assassin?"

"I doubt it. She gets others to do the dirty work. She is shrewd, calculating, and gives attention to detail. It wouldn't surprise me if she was the leader of a conspiracy, but she's much too smart to be an assassin."

"Did she oppose this high-speed rail system?" Jack asked.

"Oh, yes. This link to the United States was something she could not support."

"Were you surprised she was in the crowd?" Lou asked the obvious question.

"Absolutely. I thought she had moved on. I mean, that was the idea, to get her out of the public eye in Ottawa."

"And yet she was here. I noticed she had a media credential at the East Lansing event," Jack said, looking over his notes.

"She was not on the approved media list. I don't know how she got there in the first place. Guess our security was loose."

"She obviously didn't shoot the security officer who arrested her. So, if she is involved, she's not alone."

"That doesn't surprise me at all. As I said, she's a rebel."

"Yes, and I don't doubt that she's in a group carrying out this attack on me and disabling my security officer," the Prime Minister concluded.

Jack excused himself and went to the media car. The Victory Ride had not started for Battle Creek because of the investigation of the Taser attacks. Jack used his cell phone; and after getting the number of the Winnipeg newspaper, he dialed it.

"Good morning. Winnipeg Free Press. How may I direct your call?"

"I'd like to speak to your Editor-In-Chief."

"He's not available at the moment. Is there someone else who could help you?"

"I'd like to talk to the editor who supervises the work of reporter Shelly Westbrook."

"That would be Susan Northrup. I'll put you through."

"Thank you."

"Sue Northrup, how may I help you?"

"This is Jack Kelly, calling from Michigan."

"A reporter, no doubt," Susan began. "What newspaper do you work for?"

"I'm not a reporter. I'm calling to find out about Shelly Westbrook's assignment to cover the Victory Ride."

"Miss Westbrook has not been assigned to the Victory Ride," Sue said emphatically. "She is a guest of the Canadian Air Force on a flight to Toronto and back to cover our government's ability to respond to terrorism. She called to report that her pilot was ordered to land in Michigan and that she went to the local newspaper office."

"I see. How might I reach her?" Jack asked.

"By cell phone usually, but she's on a military jet, and I don't think you can reach her. If I were you, I'd leave a message on her voice mail. She checks for messages often. She's due back in the office tomorrow morning; her story is to be on my desk by ten a.m."

"Thank you," Jack replied. "Please put me through to her voice mail. Thank you for talking with me."

Jack said when he heard the beep, "Sorry to miss you. Please call me at your convenience." He left his number and hung up.

Lou continued to talk with the Prime Minister and his staff until a limo pulled up next to the train. With armed guards surrounding them, the Prime Minister and each member of his staff exited the train after farewells to President Fortner and Governor Halloran. With a police escort, the limo accessed nearby U.S. 127 north to I-69 and then sped east toward Canada.

With the Victory Ride idle at the East Lansing Amtrak station, Lou and Jack began to plan with security personnel for the President and the Governor.

Lou began. "By now you think the threat was clearly Canadian-based?"

"That's the logical conclusion, given the activity so far," Marcia Ludlow said.

"In my opinion, that was a 'warm-up' act for something yet to come," Lou reasoned.

"Based on what, Mr. Searing?" Marcia asked.

"Based on the fact that this Victory Ride is proceeding. If the assassin wanted the Prime Minister dead, he certainly could have killed him in Lapeer. Firearms are quite accurate, and I assume that the assassin was a marksman. Like our SWAT team members, he wouldn't miss a non-moving target."

"But the assassin or conspirators didn't know that the Ride would continue," Lou pointed out. "Besides, if we had cancelled, they couldn't commit any other crime. That was their calculated risk and they guessed right, that the Ride would continue. I still believe the assassination attempt in Lapeer was the warm-up act."

"I agree with Lou," Jack said. "I called the Winnipeg Free Press, and Shelly's editor said she was to be on a Canadian fighter jet for a story on military preparedness for a terrorist attack on a major city. She said Shelly called in from the Lansing State Journal office."

"If you're right, Lou, I suppose you recommend this ride stop here," Col. Cellar reasoned.

"Of course. We have two injuries; how many more signals do we need?"

"Once again, I vehemently oppose stopping now," the Governor began. "I believe the threat and the following events are Canadian-related. Now that it's only the President and me, I don't see why we shouldn't continue. I understand crowds are enormous in Battle Creek, Kalamazoo, and Niles. A film crew is documenting this ride because of the expectations for this project to reinvent Michigan. There's no better time to celebrate our good fortune with the President of the United States." He looked to the President, who simply nodded his approval.

While discussion continued regarding the Victory Ride, Susan Northrup of the Winnipeg Free Press called Winnipeg Air Force Base. "I'm calling for the status of the flight to Toronto piloted by Col. Stocker and carrying a member of my staff, Shelly Westbrook."

"One moment, please. I need to obtain permission to grant your request."

In a matter of seconds the flight director came on the line. "That flight was directed to land in Lansing, Michigan. The plane landed and within an hour was ordered to resume the mission. Your reporter was on board to Lansing, but she left the airport to visit the local paper. When Col. Stocker called her to return, she did not respond."

"So we don't know her location at the moment."

"Correct."

"And Col. Stocker is where?" Susan continued questioning.

"In Canadian airspace, carrying out his training mission."

CHAPTER NINE

Governor Halloran decided to contact Governor Wright. His secretary, Rose Simons placed the call from the Capitol. "Hi, Janet, Governor Halloran would like a moment to speak with Governor Wright. Is he available?"

"He's with the Lt. Governor. I will page him. Is this an emergency?"

"I'm not sure, but I doubt it."

"You can hold, but I can't predict how long he'll be," Janet said. "I really don't want to bother him. He's not in a good mood. The House and Senate are arguing about the budget."

"Then don't interrupt him, Janet. Please ask him to call Governor Halloran when he gets a minute."

"Will do, Rose. How are things in Michigan?"

"Today is our Victory Ride. The President is crossing Michigan, celebrating the high-speed rail project."

"Oh yes, that's right. A big day for Michigan," Janet replied. "Good luck, and I'll keep my fingers crossed that it goes smoothly."

"Well, we've had a couple of incidents, but the Governor wants to continue."

"Our days never lack for excitement, do they?" Janet asked. "Oops, he just walked in. I'll put him on."

"Good morning, sir. Please hold for Governor Halloran," Rose said.

Governor Halloran picked up the phone. "Hi, friend. What's this I hear about you driving 85 mph coming into my state?"

"I've no time for games, Rollie. The House and Senate are fighting tooth and nail, and I'm certainly not in Michigan. I'm in Jefferson City trying to broker a compromise."

"Really! A state police trooper indicated he stopped your vehicle in southwest Michigan this morning. There were four occupants, and the man in the passenger seat claimed to be you. He maintained he had immunity from Michigan's traffic laws."

"Wasn't me, my driver, my car, or my colleagues. You've got some 'Show Me' imposters on your hands. By the way, I saw you on TV this morning. A big day for Michigan. Regards to you and President Fortner."

"I'll pass them on. Thanks for taking time to talk with me."

"Certainly. Let me know when you find out who's playing 'Governor for a Day.'"

Lou requested that he and Jack leave the Victory Ride in East Lansing. "I really don't think there is anything we can do confined to the train, Governor. We plan to move along to Battle Creek. We'll be in touch if we learn anything and trust you'll do the same."

"Yes, definitely," The Governor replied. "Thanks for all of your help, Lou."

Jack arranged for a rental car to be brought to the Amtrak station. Once it arrived, Lou headed for U.S. 127. "We're going to the General Aviation Terminal," he informed Jack.

"Why? We won't find anyone there, Lou," Jack predicted.

"Electricity."

"Electricity?" Jack repeated, puzzled. "I'm not following."

"It flows in a circular fashion, and people are the same way."

"How so?" Jack asked, still confused.

"Shelly came into Michigan doing a story on military strategy in a terrorist attack. My guess is she's gone back to the airport, hoping someone can get her back to Winnipeg."

"A long shot—but the airport isn't far from here, and we've nothing else to do," Jack said. "Except a meal, I hope. It seems like forever since I sank my teeth into something substantial."

"I'll take care of that. But, first let's see if Shelly Westbrook is at the terminal."

As Lou drove through the intersection of Grand River and Hagadorn Road, Jack spotted Traverse Bay Pie Company. "There goes my lunch!"

"Oh, okay, Jack. I suppose we can risk a few minutes."

They discussed the case as they ate salads followed by slices of strawberry pie à la mode.

"I've never felt so much in the dark about a case before," Lou mused. "We're dealing with the threat to the Victory Ride, but nothing has fallen together neatly, if you know what I mean."

"I guess I don't know what you mean," Jack admitted.

"In our other cases, there was a murder and we investigated. In this case, it isn't that cut and dried."

"So, this time we're sitting around waiting for a crime to be committed so we can solve it?" Jack reasoned.

"Yes, or even better, so we can prevent it."

"What do you expect to happen, Lou?"

"I don't mean to think negatively, but I expect big trouble."

"Like a bomb blast?" Jack asked.

"Yes, or a river bridge blowing up when the train crosses, or a bombing from an aircraft, or an Old-West ambush. We assume the Governor and President will be the targets."

"That's a lot of negative thinking," Jack admitted.

"Well, you asked."

"Have you suggested that all bridges be inspected for explosives, or that the Air Force be alert to planes over the rails, or extra security be brought on the train to guard against an ambush?"

"No, the Secret Service knows what it is doing, and the Governor is set in his ways: he thinks everything will be fine. It might be, and I hope it turns out that way. He has in mind that this celebration is chiseled in stone, and there's nothing to worry about. That leaves us to do the wondering and worrying."

"Guess we need to act on your possibilities in hopes we can protect the Victory Ride from some catastrophe," Jack replied.

"I take it your stomach is full and you're happy," remarked Lou. "Can we get back to work now?"

Jack smiled, put his hands flat on the table, and replied, "Up and at 'em!" With that, they went back to their rental car.

The state police were on the lookout for the Lincoln with the Missouri plates. They guesstimated where the car might be, based on the location of the traffic stop. If the vehicle had not stopped, it could be somewhere around Jackson. However, if the men's destination was Kalamazoo or Battle Creek, the car would be off I-94 by now.

A be-on-the-lookout bulletin was issued, with emphasis on the possibility that the vehicle could be in Kalamazoo or Battle Creek. The vehicle also could have turned north or south at U.S. 131, just west of Kalamazoo.

As Lou pulled up to General Aviation, Jack scanned the tarmac and saw no Canadian fighter jet. Lou parked and suggested that Jack see if Shelly was in the terminal, so Jack approached the man behind the counter in the empty waiting area.

"Hello. Nice day for flying."

"Yes, it is, how may I help you?"

"I'm trying to locate this woman." Jack brought out a photo of Shelly Westbrook taken from crowd shots of the media section at East Lansing.

The man nodded. "She was in earlier—arrived with a pilot in the Canadian Air Force. I think she was a reporter for a newspaper."

"Have you seen her in the last half-hour?" Jack asked.

"No."

"And, the pilot has obviously left," Jack reasoned.

"Yes, he was ordered to continue his mission. I got the impression he tried to reach her, but he couldn't wait any longer, so he left."

"OK, thanks."

"Who are you, by the way?" the clerk asked.

"I'm Jack Kelly. I work with detective Lou Searing." Jack offered a card.

"Is there a problem with this woman?" the clerk asked.

"I wouldn't say 'a problem,' but we'd like to talk with her."

"OK, you want me to call you if she comes in?"

"Yes, thanks."

As Jack turned to walk out the door, Shelly rushed in. Jack turned to the man behind the counter, who nodded, indicating she was the woman Jack sought.

Waiting in the car, Lou was talking to Tina Block, editor of the Lansing State Journal. "Yes, she came in to check the wire for news. We told her about the Victory Ride, and she wanted to see it. So, I gave her a media pass and we took her to the Amtrak station."

"Did she know the Prime Minister would be in East Lansing this morning?"

"Yes, I'm sure knew."

"Any idea where she is now?" Lou asked.

"None. We took her to the event, and I haven't seen her since. She didn't mention anything about a conflict, nothing at all."

"Thanks, if she shows up, please give me a call." Lou gave Tina his phone number and hung up.

Jack walked quickly to the car and informed Lou that Shelly was inside. "I'll take it from here," Lou said. "You're welcome to come along if you wish."

"I always learn from you, so I'd like to."

While Jack and Lou were talking, Shelly continued to converse with the clerk in the General Aviation Terminal.

"Your pilot left without you," the clerk said to Shelly.

"I figured. Is there any way for you to contact him?"

"You will have to contact his base and talk to his superior."

Lou dialed the phone number for Col. Cellar.

"Hello, Lou. What have you got?"

"The whereabouts of Shelly Westbrook. I know she was under arrest by Canadian Security, so I have an obligation to inform them, through you, that she's in the General Aviation Terminal in Lansing. I'll intervene if you want me to, but I have no authority to arrest anyone."

"I'll contact Canadian authorities and see what they would like us to do. Please stay on the line."

"Will do."

After a few moments, he heard, "Lou?"

"Yes, go ahead."

"I'm advised that the Canadian officials will handle this themselves. If they miss her in Lansing, they know she's going to Winnipeg, and they can confront her there. They ask that you let me know if and when she leaves the terminal in Lansing."

"Okay. This is a huge mistake, but I guess I have to follow orders," Lou said with a sigh.

"A mistake, why?"

"Because she may know what's planned for the rest of the Victory Ride, and she'll likely slip out of the country."

"I understand, but we'll do what Canada wants. Shelly is their citizen, wanted by their authorities."

Shelly Westbrook used the General Aviation phone to call Susan, her editor in Winnipeg.

"It's a long story," Shelly sighed, "but I'm okay, and I've done nothing to embarrass myself or the newspaper. I just need to get out of Michigan and home. Can Col. Stocker pick me up on his way back to Winnipeg? If not, how can I get back?"

"I'm thankful you're okay," Susan began. "I'll contact the air base to see if Col. Stocker can return to Lansing to pick you up."

"Thank you very much!"

"You're welcome. Stay on the line while I try to get a definite answer for you."

Shelly tapped her fingers on the counter nervously while she waited.

"Shelly, are you there?"

"Yes, I am."

"Col. Stocker is about to land in Winnipeg and won't be returning to Michigan for you. Since you left the terminal and weren't reachable regarding the plane's departure, getting back to Winnipeg is your responsibility."

"But I have no U.S. currency, and I have no passport."

"Ouch! That could be problematic. Listen, we'll arrange for a rental vehicle. Watch the speed limit, be very careful, and cross into Canada at Sault Ste. Marie. I'll contact the Border Patrol to explain your problem and arrange for them to let you in. Once you're on Canadian soil, we'll send you money for overnight expenses. In the meantime, I'll figure out how to get you to Winnipeg."

"Thanks ever so much, Susan."

"It shouldn't take long to get a rental vehicle.

"That's right. And, I'll need money for gas and food."

"Put the man at General Aviation on the phone. I'll arrange a $100 loan. He'll give you the money. Then get in the rental car and head north."

"Thanks, Susan. Here is the man from General Aviation."

Shelly waited while Susan worked out an arrangement for the loan. After the phone call ended, the man left momentarily, returning to hand her five crisp twenty-dollar bills. She thanked him and walked outside to wait for the rental car.

The Lincoln with Missouri plates left I-94 at the 73 mile exit. It turned north then east and onto the campus of Western Michigan University. The road eventually took them into downtown Kalamazoo and into a network of closed roads and detours set up for the Victory Ride; festivities were due to begin in about an hour. Two of the men got out near downtown, disappearing into the mass of people, while the remaining two drove off, presumably to find a place to park.

Lou considered how best to deal with Shelly. The law did not prohibit him from talking to her, and he couldn't let a key player in the Victory Ride drama walk away. He turned to Jack. "I've informed the authorities where she is, but my duty ends there. I can't pass up this opportunity."

Lou got out of the car and approached the reporter, "Shelly Westbrook, Winnipeg Free Press reporter—is that right?"

Shelly showed no fear, only curiosity. "Yes. Do I know you?"

"No, but I attended the Victory Ride celebration in East Lansing and saw you in the media section. Guess the event is pretty important if a journalist of your stature covers it."

"Yes, it is important—at least for those who think the high-speed rail system might save Michigan. And you are?" Shelly said, hand outstretched.

"Lou Searing, private investigator," Lou replied. "Can I help you? You seem a bit anxious, and it's a bit odd you should be here alone."

"I'm okay, thank you. I'm stranded, is all."

"You're about the age of my daughter, and if she were alone looking anxious, I would appreciate a gentleman offering help. Are you sure there's nothing I can do for you, Miss Westbrook?"

"I'm waiting for a rental car, and I need to drive to Sault Ste. Marie. Directions from my editor in Winnipeg," she explained.

"A long drive, but the weather is good and the scenery easy on the eyes."

"I just thought of something that may be a problem," Shelly replied, shifting her weight from one foot to the other.

"What's that?" Lou asked.

"I can't drive over the Mackinac Bridge. I get dizzy going over high bridges."

"Oh, they have a driver-assistance program," Lou replied. "You just ask for an escort, and someone will drive you over. A lot of people feel like you do."

"But, I can't make contact with anyone. I must drive directly to the Canadian border."

"Well then, there is something I can do for you," Lou replied.

"Oh, but the bridge is four or five hours away," Shelly said, thinking that Lou meant to escort her into the Upper Peninsula. "I would never expect someone to do that."

"The man in the car, my assistant, Jack, has the time to go with you. We'd be glad to help, and it seems you really need to get home."

"That is very kind." Shelly thought for a moment. *This man seems like an angel. Maybe I should simply say 'thank you.'* Then she said, "If it's not too inconvenient, I guess I could accept your kindness. Once I'm home, I can reimburse you for your time."

"That won't be necessary." Lou thought, *Well, what a tangled web I'm getting myself into. I'm not only assisting a fugitive, but helping her out of the U.S., where she may be guilty of a crime.* "I'll go talk to Jack."

Lou returned to Jack. "I need you to drive Miss Westbrook to Sault Ste. Marie, Canada."

"You're kidding!"

"No, she needs help and we need information."

"Won't we be committing a crime?" Jack asked.

"What crime?" Lou asked.

"What crime?" Jack asked aghast. "How about knowingly assisting someone wanted for a crime, someone who probably has no passport."

"I'll deal with law enforcement," Lou insisted. "We can't pass up this opportunity, Jack! You and I know that fifteen minutes in a car with a stranger yields a basketful of information. Can you imagine what you might learn in six hours?"

"I'll drive her to Canada, Lou. I just hope I'm not involved in a shootout along the way or at the border."

"Nothing to worry about. Come on, I'll introduce you."

After they left, Lou, as promised, called Col. Cellar to report her departure.

The Canadian authorities who were with the Prime Minister decided not to try and apprehend Shelly Westbrook. She would eventually get back to Winnipeg, where they could take her into custody. Tracking and arresting her in the U.S.A. could be problematic; laws were complex, and the reality was that the U.S. might not cooperate in extradition procedures.

CHAPTER TEN

The Victory Ride slowly pulled out of the East Lansing Amtrak station and began the longest leg of the trip. Next stop was Battle Creek, cereal capital of the world, and then the train would head west to Kalamazoo. On the route was a bridge crossing the Kalamazoo River. If the conspirators had planted a bomb there and destroyed the train, the Victory Ride might become the 21st Century's Challenger. People would likely come from all over the world to see where a fourth U.S. President had been killed.

Sheriff's deputies had inspected the trestle earlier in the day and determined that the bridge was safe. They didn't anticipate conspirators setting their explosives within an hour of the train's expected arrival at the trestle.

With the Prime Minister and entourage heading to Windsor, and Jack and Shelly on their way to Sault Ste. Marie, Lou took time to reassess his situation. The Governor's security detail was doing a good job of keeping Lou briefed on what they learned. Lou mentally put the pieces of the puzzle on a table in his mind. Significant facts pointed to an elaborate conspiracy.

In Lapeer, the wounding of the Canadian Prime Minister was either a missed assassination attempt or a portent of things to come. A second indication was the unexplained presence of Shelly Westbrook, Canadian activist and troublemaker for the Prime Minister. A third was the disabling of the security officer who had arrested Shelly in East Lansing. A possible fourth factor was the "Missouri contingent," whose member claimed to be the Governor of Missouri. Lou didn't know whether he'd identified all of the conspirators, but they all appeared to be inexperienced rookies, at best.

Jack and Shelly were driving past Alma. "If Lou were here he would be talking your ear off about Alma College. He spent two years of his life on this campus, has fond memories of playing on the golf team. They were good years, but studying and intense reading were not Lou's forté. He decided to go into special education and transferred to Western Michigan University. Anyway, you can be thankful he's not here."

Shelly smiled. "I went to McGill University in Montreal. I did read and study very hard, actually. I credit McGill for guiding me into journalism and giving me a good start in the job market."

"I went to Aquinas College in Grand Rapids," Jack said. "I had a good experience there and enjoyed it. I loved numbers, which explains why I became an accountant."

"I've never heard of that school—or Alma either."

"Can't say I'm surprised. They're way out of your backyard. I haven't heard of many small independent colleges in Canada."

"Aren't you curious about what I am doing in Michigan, driving a rental car to Canada?" Shelly asked, abruptly changing the subject.

"Of course, but I don't want to be nosy. I figure if you want to tell me something, you will."

"I'm usually the one asking questions, but I imagine you have more than a few."

"Lou asked me to go with you across the Mackinac and the International Bridges. And, that's what I'm doing. I've no need to know what you don't want to share," Jack believed he would get more details if he didn't probe. On the other hand, the Victory Ride was moving, and if Shelly's knowledge could save lives, he wished she'd open up a bit.

Presently, she sighed and began to talk. "What do you think about this new high-speed rail system?"

"Sounds great," Jack responded. "Michigan needs jobs and a new industry, and this could be it. We have solid agriculture and tourist economies, but we've lost considerable manufacturing. This rail initiative gives us a chance to provide leadership in a new industry, while employing thousands. I, for one, think it's great. How about you?"

"I agree with you and the same holds true for Ontario."

"Then why would some not want this to move forward?" Jack asked.

"Change, Jack. People can't handle change."

"But this is good change," Jack reasoned.

"Doesn't matter—change upsets the apple cart. It's human nature to want to stay with what is known, what's predictable. High-speed rail will impact communities, shipment of goods, and the transportation of people. Add government to the mix, and it gets messy."

Jack decided to take the plunge. "Why were you arrested in East Lansing?"

"I honestly don't know—I wasn't breaking any law. Well, I didn't have my passport with me, but nobody knew that. I was present by a fluke of circumstances."

"But someone considered you a threat?" Jack asked.

"The Prime Minister hates my guts, so when he saw me, he probably decided to make my life miserable."

"'Hates your guts'—that's pretty strong language."

"When I was based in Ottawa, I led a number of what he considered radical social responses to government intervention into the lives of citizens. Demonstrations I organized were costly to the government. In a few instances they changed policy, but not enough to make a major difference."

"Did you object to his endorsement of the high-speed rail system in Ontario?"

"I wrote a few articles in which I proposed that it made more sense for Canada to build the system from Quebec City to Toronto on its own. I guess I was being nationalistic, but I'm a Canadian journalist and I wrote what I truly believe."

"So, you became an obstacle for the Prime Minister, who favored the Toronto-to-Chicago route."

"Exactly."

"The security officer who was disabled escorting you away from the crowd—do you know who may have attacked him?"

"I'm not going there, Jack."

"Because there is a conspiracy?"

"No comment."

"Okay, but I think you've answered my question anyway," Jack concluded.

"I didn't say there is a conspiracy—you should be able to figure that out for yourself. However, I will say that the Prime Minister's decision was not popular with people with money in positions of power."

"Uh-huh. That officer who arrested you. He was shot, or had some kind of episode, and collapsed. You sought medical care and then slipped into the crowd."

"I never said he was shot."

"No. You didn't. I don't know whether his injury was part of a plan or if the collapse was due to a natural cause."

"I need some food. I'm getting off at this exit. Will you eat?" Shelly asked, ending the discussion.

"Sure, why not."

As he sat in Blondie's Barn restaurant in Haslett, Lou's cell phone rang. It was Col. Cellar calling from the Victory Ride, and Lou answered immediately, "Lou, we've got a problem here. We need you."

"Where are you?"

"Charlotte."

"I can be there in 30 minutes. What's the problem?"

"The President got a call from the CIA. They believe that a terrorist attack is imminent because the President is confined to the train and can't communicate with people in D.C."

"That's ridiculous!" Lou exclaimed. "No matter where the President is, he has access to whomever he wants. His team can't help him with this?"

"All I know is that the country is likely in imminent danger, and the President is on a train in farm country."

"And you want my help?" Lou asked incredulously. "What can I do in this situation?"

"Find someone skilled in ham radio technology and have…" The phone went dead.

Lou went to his car and turned on the radio, searching for a station with news; he was shocked by what he heard. "Possibly the result of a terrorist attack, a widespread disruption of the national power grid beginning in the New York area is sweeping across the country. Electrical power is failing faster than anyone can respond to the emergency."

Lou was at a loss for what to do. The power was out, he had no means of communicating, and he couldn't drive because the traffic lights were out. He immediately thought of Carol and wondered where she was. He went back into Blondie's, ordered a cup of coffee and waited with other nervous customers.

Lou was approached by a couple who seemed to recognize him. "Hi, Lou."

"Oh my goodness, Randy and Julie. Good to see you."

"The power is out, as you already know, so we parked our motorcycles and came in thinking a hot cup of coffee might be available," Randy said.

"Do you still ride your Harley, Lou?" Julie asked.

"On rare occasions. Carol is quite happy the bike has found a permanent and dusty place in the garage."

"You must be working on a case," Randy said realizing Lou was far from home.

"As a matter of fact I am."

"Why are we not surprised?" Julie asked.

The three friends recalled memories of meeting one another at a motorcycle event in Ohio. Both had Michigan tags, so they struck up a conversation and the friendship started."

"Listen, get back to work. Good to see you, Lou. We'll hope our paths cross again."

"Sooner than later," Lou replied. "Blondie will have some hot coffee for you I'm sure. Have a safe journey."

The blackout was sudden and extensive. It seemed as though someone had flipped a switch off over the entire east coast. The second area to have no electricity was the south. The third was the Great Lakes States and the Mid-west. Engineers at the major power grid stations were unable to stop the increasing outages that spread like a fog coming off a lake.

Everyone affected assumed it was a simple power outage; that within a minute, or fifteen minutes, hopefully no more than an hour, power would be restored. One problem was lack of communication. People depended on radio, television, and the Internet to give them news of this nature. But there was no way to find out what was going on or the reason for the blackout.

The one saving grace was that it was mid-day, so the country wasn't plunged into darkness. Planes in the air could land because of emergency airport generators and new procedures followed by air traffic controllers who had had a taste of quickly guiding planes out of the air on 9-11.

Meanwhile, power grids continued to shut down from east to west. California was beginning to experience the electrical outage. Just as engineers were beginning to think Canada might avoid the power loss, the lights went out in Ottawa, Montreal, and Toronto.

People didn't immediately go into a panic mode, because most simply thought their local power station had a temporary outage. Whenever people tried to place calls, they heard silence as they did when they turned on their TVs and radios. They went to their automobiles hoping to use the electricity created in their car batteries. While the radios in their cars worked, there was nothing to listen to for lack of transmission of any radio signal. It was becoming obvious that the problem was bigger than a local substation.

Jack and Shelly found themselves in a Big Boy Restaurant when the lights went out. They figured the place needed a new fuse or if a wider area was affected, a power outage was the culprit. They finished their meal and got back on the road.

The President's staff was able to use the Amateur Radio Emergency Service to connect with Fort Custer in Battle Creek, who in turn connected the President to the White House. The President was assured that he was in no danger and that this disruption of power was not the result of terrorism, but a temporary problem, probably the result of a solar flare.

In Kalamazoo, city police found the Lincoln Continental with Missouri plates parked on South Street, several blocks from the Amtrak station. Because of road closures and so many people hoping to see the President and the Governor, this had been the closest place to park.

The officer put the license number into the computer system in his squad car and discovered the number matched the vehicle pulled over by the state trooper several hours earlier. The officer learned that the vehicle was registered to a Mr. Vincent Maglioto, and no tickets had been issued in the past. A glance into the car showed nothing of interest. All the police could do was wait for the owner to return.

The Kalamazoo police officer took several photos of the vehicle. He noticed a lot of dust on the body near the tires, to be expected on an SUV, but not on a new luxury automobile.

Shelly and Jack continued to drive north, unaware that the entire country was without power because they didn't pull off the four-lane. They continued their conversation.

"For the life of me, I can't understand why you might be a threat to the Victory Ride," Jack said.

"The Prime Minister had to save face, to let Canadians know he's in charge. I was in the front row of the media section, and he would not be upstaged. The best way to avoid that was to have me arrested and have the other media make a big deal out of the arrest."

"I guess that makes sense. But this officer escorting you had some kind of a medical issue. You tried to get medical attention, then walked away and eventually ended up at General Aviation."

"That's right. Was I supposed to run up to an officer of the law and say, 'I'm under arrest, but the arresting officer fainted. Will you take over?' I may be a bit slow on the uptake, but I'm not stupid, and I have enough common sense to make a selfish decision—like escaping."

Jack noted Shelly's comment in relation to the officer not being shot. *I didn't say he was shot, did I? She wanted me to know she knew he wasn't shot.* But she really couldn't know, at least not in Jack's reasoning, which implied she likely knew what really happened. And if that were the case, she had to have been involved in the action and whatever was planned. Jack noted his observation, not only to be sure to remember it, but to tell Lou what he had heard.

Jack considered the facts another way: perhaps the arresting officer was part of the conspiracy, and his role was to allow Shelly to get away. If that were true, the security team for the Prime Minister had a different mission than to protect the leader of Canada.

Jack thought it best to check in with Lou, but something was not right. His phone showed power, but the phone was dead. He was within sight of a relay tower. He turned on the car radio and although the lights came on, there was no signal.

"Something's awry," Jack remarked.

"Power out?" Shelly asked.

"Well, my phone doesn't work, and the radio has no power. I've noticed several semis have pulled to the side of the road.

The weather is good, so there is no logical reason for them to pull off. It seems like they would wait to pull into a rest area."

"Maybe they know something we don't," Shelly offered.

"They have CB radios. Maybe they're working. Let's pull into the next rest area, find a trucker, and see what he knows."

"Fine with me."

Lou was beside himself with frustration. He couldn't drive; traffic was in gridlock because signals were out, and he couldn't pump gas if he needed it. He couldn't contact anyone and he had no idea what was happening on the Victory Ride. He couldn't tell whether this commotion was the result of overload of the system or if, in fact, terrorists had disrupted all American activity.

Lou really had no choice but to stay put in Blondie's Haslett restaurant until calmer heads prevailed and either fixed the system or brought order to mass confusion.

The President was successfully in touch with his leadership team in the White House. "What is this all about? Do we know?" President Fortner asked.

"We do know it is not terrorism, Mr. President," replied Vice President Richardson.

"'Not terrorism'—I assume that you mean not any kind of terrorism, either within or outside of the country?"

"That is correct," the Vice President stated with authority. "It's a massive failure of our electrical grid. Scientists predicted solar-flare activity, but they thought it wouldn't be disruptive. Well, it is disruptive."

"Didn't we learn anything from a similar episode several years ago in the eastern states?" President Fortner asked, frustrated with not being in D.C. during this major problem.

"Apparently not much, Mr. President."

"What's the timeline for correcting this? How long until people get power?"

"One good thing from the last outage is they know how best to restore the system."

"How long till the people get power?" The President asked again, losing patience.

"We've been told one to two hours, max," Vice President Richardson replied.

"Good. I want all governmental units informed that this is a short disruption and that we should soon be back to normal."

"Yes, sir."

"And, most important, I want the country to know that we are acting on this efficiently and without delay. We won't have another Katrina. Am I clear?"

"Yes, sir."

"And I want a TV crew here in Charlotte, Michigan ASAP. As soon as power is restored, I need to assure the people that I'm on top of this."

"Yes, Mr. President. Please inform the Prime Minister this problem exists throughout Canada as well."

"He is not on the Victory Ride."

"He's not? Where is he?" the Vice President asked.

"Returning to Ottawa. He was wounded, as you know, and he wanted to get back to Ottawa. I assume the Secretary of State has informed other national leaders that our lack of power is not a terrorist threat. Correct?"

"Yes, Mr. President."

"I've just been informed that a TV crew is here already. You're fast, very fast."

"Can't take credit for it, sir," the Vice President replied.

"Excuse me for a second." The President turned to listen to the Governor.

"WILX in Lansing took a chance on finding you. Here's your opportunity to talk to the public, once power is restored."

The President nodded and turned back to his conversation. "I'll stay on the line for other developments."

"Yes, sir," Vice President Richardson replied. "We'll serve in any way you direct."

"Thank you."

CHAPTER ELEVEN

Shelly and Jack had barely gotten up to the speed limit when Shelly glanced at her rear-view mirror and saw a state police vehicle coming toward her at a high rate of speed.

Her speedometer read seventy-three mph. Granted, she was over the limit, but only by a few miles an hour, and she certainly wasn't likely to be pulled over. She slowed and moved off the road, thinking the vehicle might whiz by to apprehend a speeder, or assist with an accident up the road.

The cruiser slowed as it approached her rental car. A state trooper pulled up behind Shelly, exited his vehicle, and walked to the side of the car.

"What do you think this is about?" Shelly asked Jack.

"Fairly obvious. You were under arrest, and they lost you. You've been tracked to this point, and the trooper will arrest you again."

"Can you help me?" Shelly asked in an almost begging tone.

"I don't see how I can. I have no authority. I can assure him you've broken no driving laws, but that's about it."

The officer walked up to the driver's side of the car and Shelly rolled down the window.

"Are you Shelly Westbrook?" the trooper asked.

"Yes, but Officer, I was not breaking any traffic law. I was only going about seventy-three and that hardly requires you stopping me."

"Miss Westbrook, come with me, please. You can cooperate or you can resist, but that would be a big mistake. My vehicle's camera will capture any movement and the microphone will record anything you say."

"Officer," Jack said. "She was not speeding. If a brake light isn't working, we can fix that in no time. I don't suggest she resist, but I can tell any judge that Miss Westbrook was not violating any traffic law when you pulled her over."

"As I said, Miss Westbrook, you are requested to come with me. Or I can call for backup, and we'll physically remove you from the vehicle."

"Am I under arrest? Does a Canadian citizen have any rights? Can I contact an attorney before deciding not to resist?"

"No, I am not arresting you, and yes, you have rights. But I recommend you do as I ask."

Shelly looked at Jack who simply shrugged his shoulders as if to say, "Guess you had better go."

"Shall I come with her?" Jack asked.

"No, you are to return the rental car to Lansing," the officer said firmly.

Shelly got out of her car. "Do you need to search me, or do I just get in your vehicle?"

"You likely have no weapon. You have no purse, no ID, and no right be in the United States. Please get in the back seat of my vehicle and put the seat belt on. You, Mr. Kelly, should turn around at the next exit and return to Lansing. Thank you for your cooperation."

Jack nodded, got out and walked around the back of the car, entered the driver side, adjusted his seat belt and drove onto the highway, looking for an exit to head south.

A police officer at the Battle Creek Amtrak station walked up the platform steps carrying a bullhorn and raised it to speak to the crowd. "May I have your attention please? Your attention please! The Victory Ride is currently in Charlotte. The electrical outage covers the entire country, but is not a terrorist attack. Power should be restored in the next hour or so. The Victory Ride will resume, and the President and the Governor should arrive in about an hour-and-a-half. You are welcome to stay here. The Kellogg Company has donated bottled water, which will be here shortly. If you choose to leave, please understand that traffic signals are not working, and there are traffic jams at most major intersections."

The crowd mumbled, as everyone had something to say about their predicament and the frustration in not being able to reach family members. Most people decided to find shelter from the spring sun and wait.

The electrical grids were once again providing electricity throughout the east coast, and, like the "wave" in a football stadium, electricity was gradually restored from the Atlantic to the Pacific.

People immediately turned on their televisions to find out what had happened. Each of the major networks had a report. Scott Pelley on CBS, Brian Williams on NBC, and Diane Sawyer on ABC each summarized the crisis after receiving reports from correspondents throughout the country, and even from foreign capitals.

The reports were like a broken record. Each newscaster accurately explained the cause of the blackout, as well as the steps that had been taken to correct it. Each network gave time to the President for his comments. On CBS, Scott Pelley said, "We have a message from President Fortner in Charlotte, Michigan."

"Thank you, Scott. Well, the blackout was a scare. In our age of terrorism, an attack in some form is always a possibility.

Like most Americans, I thought the worst, but I am relieved that this was not a terrorist attack but rather a problem in the electrical grid system caused by a solar flare. A similar blackout occurred along the East Coast a few years ago, and like all of you, I presumed the problem had been solved. I assure you that at all times, government officials were on top of this matter. I will appoint a Presidential Committee to study this event and to recommend steps to be taken to assure that this will not happen again. I will expect this report in a timely fashion, and you will be informed of the committee's recommendations. I hope you are able to resume your activities in a safe manner, free from concerns. Good afternoon."

"Thank you for those reassuring words, Mr. President. Now, for details of the event and its effect on citizens, we turn to our CBS affiliate in Baltimore..."

The only one removed from the turmoil was the Prime Minister. His small entourage, invisible to the public, moved along toward Detroit and the Ambassador Bridge. When the vehicle needed gas, the driver pulled off the expressway and found himself in a jam without traffic lights. Once they found the nearest filling station, they couldn't get gas, so the Prime Minister and his security team simply sat it out.

With power restored, the Victory Ride resumed toward Battle Creek. "The Ride was intended to be nothing short of a celebration, Mr. President," the Governor said, shaking his head. "I'm sorry we've encountered so many glitches."

"Yes, it's a bit more drama that I bargained for, but I wanted to celebrate with you. The rail system is a major coup for the state of Michigan and I am selfish; I need to carry Michigan in the next election—it's a true swing state. I hope the visibility and the award to Michigan will nudge the state into my column."

"I join in that hope, Mr. President. My staff will campaign vigorously for you. While I can't guarantee anything, I am confident that the Michigan electorate appreciates what you have done for them, and they'll vote for you. 'You can take it to the bank,' as they say."

As Jack headed south on U.S. 27, the trooper and Shelly continued north. The trooper exited at Clare and contacted base via his radio. The dispatcher briefed him on the restored power and gave him instructions. "Take Miss Westbrook to the Clare Regional Airport, about three miles north of Clare. Another trooper will take over there."

Lou contacted Jack on his cell to find out what he had learned from Shelly. "She's a hard nut to crack, Lou," Jack said. "I don't understand why, but a State Police trooper pulled us over south of Clare. He didn't arrest her, but he took her with him and told me to return to Lansing. I'm coming up to Mt. Pleasant at the moment, so I should be at the General Aviation terminal in about an hour."

"OK, I'll meet you there, and then we'll catch up with the Victory Ride. To be honest, I'm at a loss for what is happening. On one hand I see a conspiracy carrying out a detailed plan, which may have a disastrous ending. But on the other, I see a strange set of occurrences that might be totally unrelated."

"Well, I put my vote in the conspiracy column," Jack offered.

"You may be right."

"The enormity of it bothers me, Lou. We don't have just a coincidence or two. We have a threat, a shooting, an arrest, two security guards being Tasered, a woman on the run without a passport, a nationwide electrical blackout, and a car from Missouri allegedly carrying their Governor."

"Almost impossible to tie these things to a coherent plan to affect the Victory Ride," Lou offered.

"Not all of these may be part of the conspiracy, like the grid failure, and maybe the arrest of the woman in East Lansing, but the shooting of the Prime Minister and the Missouri vehicle could be connected."

"I agree."

The Victory Ride pulled into Battle Creek under tight security. The crowd around the Amtrak station was dotted with police. But, for the first time, everything went according to plan with no distractions. The Battle Creek Central High School Band played the *Star Spangled Banner* and *Michigan My Michigan* while the crowd awaited the appearance of the Governor and the President.

Workers had moved the podium to the middle of the platform positioned in front of the train door. The politicians could step right out onto the platform and speak from behind the protective glass.

The mayor of Battle Creek came through the crowd, walking up onto the platform. "What a special day for the city of Battle Creek!" he shouted. The crowd cheered. "Today our leaders are with us to celebrate joy in every Michiganian's heart—the promise of a new tomorrow. Just as Battle Creek leads the nation in cereal production, Michigan will soon lead the nation in the development of high-speed rail technology and manufacturing.

"You didn't come here today to hear me, but to celebrate this wonderful news. Ladies and gentlemen, boys and girls, I present the Governor of the State of Michigan, the honorable Roland Halloran."

As the Governor emerged from the train, a loud cheer went up from people gathered for a block around the Amtrak station. "Thank you, Mr. Mayor. Thank you, everyone, for coming out to greet us as we continue the Victory Ride. I'm sorry we're late. But as you have heard by now, the nation's power system shut down. But, we won't allow that to dampen our joy today. We led the nation in automobile production, and now we will lead the nation in high-speed rail. We have our President to thank for our good fortune. President Fortner believes in us and wants to see our Michigan fiscally sound. We will not let you down, Mr. President. Please give a huge Battle Creek welcome to President Alan Fortner."

The band played *Hail to the Chief,* and confetti rained down from the roof of the station. The President stepped up to the microphone to a sustained round of applause, taking notes from his suit coat pocket.

"Good afternoon, Battle Creek, cereal capital of the world! Thank you for your warm welcome. Thank you, Mr. Mayor. Thank you to Kellogg Company for providing water to people during our electrical shut-down. This kindness exemplifies the sense of community that defines America.

"I cannot add much to the comments of your mayor and your Governor, except to reiterate that my administration is committed to finding and/or creating jobs to help Americans realize the dreams of all of us: to be independent; to own a home; to send their children to college if they so choose; and to retire in comfort." Another sustained round of applause arose.

The President was pleased to see a large homemade sign: "Four More Years for President Fortner!" He gave a "thumbs-up" signal to the people around the sign in appreciation for their efforts and message.

"We're running behind schedule and we have crowds waiting for us in Kalamazoo and Niles, so we must leave. Thank you for your warm welcome. Michigan has a bright future!"

The President and the Governor retreated into the train car, the platform was removed, and the Victory Ride continued on to Kalamazoo.

The trooper did not speak to Shelly, nor did he answer her questions. She finally sat quietly, wondering what else could happen on this crazy day. The state police car pulled into the Clare airport, and they walked to a small office.

Shelly presumed she was to be deported; she prayed to go home, but she feared going to an Ottawa jail for some reason known only to the Prime Minister.

The trooper said to a man in a flight suit. "This is Shelly Westbrook. I assume she's the person you are waiting for."

"Yes, thank you, trooper. We appreciate your assistance."

"When the Royal Canadian Mounted Police ask, we always try to be helpful."

"Likewise."

Shelly said nothing, nor did she resist as she was led to a small single-prop Cessna. She climbed up onto the wing and into the passenger seat. The door closed behind her, and the pilot went around the tail of the plane and entered the pilot's seat.

Without a word, the pilot went through pre-flight protocol, fired up the engine, and taxied to the end of the single runway. As the plane slowly moved away from the airport office, Shelly tried to read the pilot's name tag. "Sergeant Robbins, is it? Would you please explain what's happening? Where are we going? Who is behind this?"

The pilot looked straight ahead. "I'm Sergeant Toby Robbins of the Royal Canadian Mounted Police. Your newspaper has asked us to fly you to Winnipeg."

"That's the best thing I've heard all day," Shelly said, enjoying a deep breath and a relaxation of almost every muscle in her body.

"Your editor and publisher heard about your dilemma and wanted you in Winnipeg as quickly as possible. Your newspaper has helped the Mounted Police on several occasions, so we agreed to fly to Michigan and bring you home."

"Wonderful," Shelly said with much relief. "I'm so grateful!"

"Thank your editor and your publisher. They're the ones who wanted you home."

The Cessna waited at the end of the runway as the pilot went over last-minute checks. He picked up his radio and informed pilots in the area that he was taking off and heading due west. As the plane went down the runway and lifted off, Shelly was five hours from home.

CHAPTER TWELVE

As the Victory Ride continued on to Kalamazoo, Lou, identifying himself as working for the federal government, contacted Stan Fedewa, Sheriff of Kalamazoo County. "Has the trestle over the Kalamazoo River been checked for explosives?"

"Yes, this morning," Sheriff Fedewa replied.

"I suggest you check it again before the train arrives."

"That isn't necessary," Stan replied. "The trestle is rather remote and hard to get to on foot. It was clean this morning, and that's good enough for me."

"Did a K-9 unit accompany those who inspected the trestle?" Lou asked.

"No. I didn't think that was necessary either."

"Well, it might be, and I suggest you re-inspect the bridge and take an explosives-detecting dog along."

"I'll consider your request."

"If that trestle blows and the train is destroyed, you'll have that on your conscience for the rest of your life."

"Listen, I don't know who you are, but every inch of rail through Kalamazoo County is game for explosives and danger. I can't imagine why you think that trestle deserves any more scrutiny than the rest of the route."

"I am not going to argue with you," Lou replied. "Just re-inspect it, and take a dog with you."

Lou ended the call.

Sheriff Fedewa thought, *Forget it. I don't have the manpower to recheck that trestle. Lou Searing? Who's he to boss me around anyway? The people of Kalamazoo County elected me sheriff, not him.*

Lou called Col. Cellar on the Victory Ride.

"I just talked to the Kalamazoo County Sheriff, asked him to re-inspect the trestle over the Kalamazoo River with an explosives-detecting dog. I got the distinct impression that he wasn't willing. Perhaps you should call and ask if he has rechecked it. If he hasn't, I strongly advise you to stop the train before the trestle. I have a gut feeling that the Victory Ride should not go over that trestle without a thorough inspection."

"I respect your gut, I'll have it inspected."

"I don't think you have much time."

"I agree."

"With everything that has happened today, I wouldn't be surprised if a bomb on that trestle was the final link in the plan."

"I'll let you know what happens."

"I'm going on to Kalamazoo. I hope to find our Missouri friends before things get going."

"Okay, Lou. Plan to board the train when we stop there."

The Cessna plane with Shelly on board continued its flight toward Winnipeg. The flight was scenic, smooth, and without incident. The pilot seemed to be more talkative than she thought necessary, compared with other times she had flown in a small aircraft. But, she wasn't a pilot and could hardly hear what he was saying because of the noise in the cockpit. All she cared about was that the plane kept heading northwest and that sooner or later, she would see the outskirts of Winnipeg.

The Prime Minister had crossed the Ambassador Bridge from Detroit to Windsor, Ontario, glad to be alive and back in his beloved Canada. His private jet, Challenger 601 built by Air Canada waited at the Windsor airport. More often than not, he would request to go somewhere other than Ottawa, as would be the case today. He had gotten a call from Col. Cellar who told him the state police had assisted the RCMP in locating Shelly Westbrook and that she was in airspace en route to Winnipeg.

Boarding the plane, he said to the pilot, "Good afternoon. I want to go to Winnipeg."

"Yes, sir."

The Prime Minister and his staff, as well as a few select members of the media, boarded the private Lear jet. The pilot informed the tower of his plan to fly directly to Winnipeg. Presently, the tower gave the pilot clearance to take off.

The plane had no sooner left the ground than the Prime Minister called Mr. William Batchelder, the leader of the Province of Manitoba. "Greetings, Bill. I am on my way to Winnipeg—should arrive late afternoon, your time. When I arrive I want to meet with your head of security. And I want you to track down Shelly Westbrook, a reporter with the Winnipeg Free Press. I want her to meet with me in an airport conference room. Sources in the United States inform me that she is en route to Winnipeg in an RCMP Cessna. I have no idea why they would ferry her from Michigan to Winnipeg, but I intend to find out."

"Will do. I'll find out where the flight is now, meet the plane, and take Miss Westbrook to safe quarters until your arrival."

"Thank you."

Mr. Batchelder called the Air Commander of the Royal Canadian Mounted Police.

"I want to locate one of your planes. It is en route from Michigan to Winnipeg and carrying Shelly Westbrook."

"One moment, please." The chain of command was followed, and soon an operator responded. "The flight you've specified is currently 4 kilometers south of our border with Minnesota."

"Please inform the pilot that in Winnipeg I will personally escort his passenger from the plane to our conference room."

"Yes, sir."

Col. Cellar called the Kalamazoo County Sheriff. "Have you rechecked the trestle as Mr. Searing asked?"

"Yes sir, but I wasn't happy about it. I don't like private citizens telling me what to do."

"I understand, but Mr. Searing seems to be on top of something," Col. Cellar replied.

"He was confronted by federal security personnel early this morning, and he went right to the Head of the FBI. He has some sort of credential that allows him access to any federal facility and to assist in any suspected federal crime."

"Really. I figured he was just a rude private investigator trying to play cop."

"Nothing could be further from the truth. He is very highly regarded, so I'm glad you took his advice. What did you find?"

"Nothing. Like I told him, it had been checked and ruled secure."

"Good. So, the trestle is safe?"

"If someone is intent on destroying the train, he could plant other explosive devices in the area. But, there is no bomb on, under, or near the trestle."

"Good job, Sheriff."

"Thanks. I need to get into town for the Victory Ride."

By now, all the major networks were covering the Victory Ride. The events of the day were no longer a secret and every network was following this story closely. To add to the drama, correspondents cited the initial threats to the Victory Ride, and the wounding of the Prime Minister. The trip seemed doomed by the electrical grid shutdown. The media hadn't learned of Lou's bomb scare concern. The train passed over the bridge smoothly and without incident.

The Victory Ride arrived at the Amtrak station on the north side of Kalamazoo, to the highest level of security. Television stations were ready to cover the event. An aura of stress on everyone responsible for the event: security, speakers, media, was dominant around the station.

On the other hand, the public figured that the dignitaries on board expected this level of law enforcement. Wherever one looked there were military, SWAT members, and uniformed officers on duty, not to mention the plain-clothes officers that blended in with the crowd. An upward glance revealed several officers on roofs near the station.

Lou was certain that the Missouri men, as he called them, were also somewhere. Was it their mission to be in the crowd, or in a position to assassinate the President of the United States?

Lou got a call from Governor Wright in Jefferson City, Missouri. "Mr. Searing, I decided to call you because I imagine every officer of the law is on duty in Kalamazoo. CNN has been covering the President since late this morning. They have all but admitted that he's in imminent danger."

"It's crazy to continue the Victory Ride, Lou offered. "They might as well have invited everyone to the county fair to watch plastic ducks waddle across a shooting gallery. If this train reaches New Buffalo before sundown with a healthy Governor and President, I'll be thankfully surprised. It will be a minor miracle. Anyway, what can I do for you?" Lou asked.

"I have some information about the men in the Continental and the man who claimed to be me."

"This is a stroke of luck. That's part of the day's drama that makes no sense."

"Missouri lobbied hard and spent millions of dollars trying to convince the federal government that the project should be awarded for a high-speed rail line from St. Louis to Kansas City. We lost, and that's politics, so we moved on to other initiatives. However, some people are poor losers, and I believe four of them drove to Michigan to seek revenge for a wrong they think was done them by the President and the Canadian Prime Minister."

"Makes sense. Sad, of course, but logical."

"Anyway, I don't know who these four are, but I have an idea about how to find them."

"What's that?" Lou asked.

"It's a sting that I saw used when I was in a police cadet program in high school."

"These sometimes work. Tell me about it."

"An official of Kalamazoo comes to the microphone before any of the dignitaries emerge. He or she says something like, 'We have a surprise for some lucky person here at the Kalamazoo Victory Ride Event. We've written down the license numbers of every vehicle within a ten-block area surrounding this Amtrak station. We put the information in a drum, and our mayor drew the lucky number. The owner of the car will win a thousand dollars through the generosity of local merchants, pleased that high-speed rail service is coming through Kalamazoo. So, if your license number is called, please identify yourself to one of our Victory Ride Kalamazoo staff. He or she can verify your license number, and a check for one thousand dollars will be issued to you at the Chamber of Commerce."

Lou was cynical. "A professional criminal wouldn't fall for the sting, Governor."

"You don't know that. The human being has lots of strings to pull. One of the four just might forget for a minute and show a reaction that you can pick up. If someone comes forward, you take him aside and do your thing."

"My thing?" Lou asked.

"You scare the pants off him. Tell him the gig is up. Tell him the President is not getting off the train until the four are in a police van."

"Nah, I don't think it'll work. I don't have enough evidence to accuse them and I don't have a thousand dollars to give them if they're innocent."

"What have you got to lose?" Governor Wright asked. "You won't bother anyone else because only these four know about their license number."

"Thank you, Governor Wright, but no thanks. I might try it if I was fairly certain these were viable suspects, but I'm not."

The train had stopped a few blocks short of the Kalamazoo station to allow dignitaries from the city, Western Michigan University, and Kalamazoo College to board and meet the President and Governor. They quickly went over the order of speaking and their places on the platform. Finally, they were alerted to the possibility of disruption of the festivities and what to do in that event. When all was set, the train slowly moved into position by the platform.

At this stop, the Western Michigan University marching band entertained the crowd. The train was behind schedule after the electrical outage and long-winded remarks from the dignitaries.

The Missouri Four were in the crowd. They easily passed through metal-detecting machines, and they were ignored by a K-9 Unit German Shepherd whose nose was working overtime. They merged with the people of Kalamazoo who had come out to witness history.

First, the Mayor of Kalamazoo welcomed the Victory Ride tour and offered glowing words about how the high-speed rail system would boost their economy. He held up two keys to the city that would be presented to the Governor and the President when they came out to speak.

The next speaker, Harold Southwell, President of Western Michigan University, stepped to the microphone and spoke with great enthusiasm. "I am pleased to be here today with a very important announcement. The Trustees of WMU have voted unanimously to establish the Western Michigan University College of Intercontinental Transportation, dedicated to the study of efficient transportation. Researchers will find ways to make travel safer and more convenient, and seek means to use high-speed rail to improve the economies of both Michigan and Canada. WMU intends to be the intellectual heart and soul of this initiative."

Watching television from his office in the Administration Building on the campus of Central Michigan University, President Orman Phillips realized he had just been upstaged. He turned to Tanya Eppinga, his administrative assistant, and asked, "Who let this opportunity get by?"

"I guess maybe we're not as forward-thinking as others in academia," Tanya replied.

"I've got to hand it to WMU," President Phillips said with a smile. "They capitalized on a great idea. Good for them, is all I can say."

"Our Trustees will want to know why you didn't come up with the idea," Tanya said.

"You're right, they will. I'll talk to our Director of Research and Innovation and see if we missed something in the Federal Register. Now every time I see that high-speed train fly by, I'll be reminded of a lost opportunity to put CMU on the cutting edge of technology for transportation."

Once President Southwell finished his speech, the Mayor introduced the Governor who said much the same as he had at the previous stops. There are only so many ways to express pride at a new opportunity for Michigan. He introduced the President, who emerged to a very warm reception. The enthusiastic crowd waved, clapped, and held up signs as the band played *For He's a Jolly Good Fellow.*

Once the applause died down, the President thanked the people for coming out. He also thanked Dr. Southwell for the creation of a new college and expressed his desire to assist in its funding. He closed by saying that, as a Yankees fan, he was proud to be in the town where Derek Jeter played high school baseball. Everyone cheered at the mention of a hometown boy who had made good on a national level.

CHAPTER THIRTEEN

Fifteen minutes after pulling into Kalamazoo, the Victory Ride departed, moving past Western Michigan University and heading for Niles with a short stop in Dowagiac. After three more stops, President Fortner would take his limousine to Air Force One, waiting at the South Bend airport. The day had been long and tiring, but the chance to be with the American people and experience genuine excitement about the future did his heart good.

While driving to Dowagiac, Lou and Jack tossed around theories on the developing case.

"I'm convinced it is a Canadian problem," Jack said.

"How so?" Lou asked, wanting to hear Jack's reasoning.

"The Royal Canadian Mounted Police is responsible for protecting the Prime Minister, but they certainly haven't done the best job of that. And, they allowed the Winnipeg journalist to get away."

"What is your take on the Missouri Four?" Lou asked.

"They have nothing to do with this Victory Ride."

"I agree, but I can't help but wonder who they are, and why they're here in Kalamazoo if they aren't involved in some way."

"My sentiments exactly," Jack replied.

"So, can I assume you have Shelly as an undercover operative working for the RCMP?"

"I'm leaning that way, yes."

"Is the Winnipeg newspaper in on this plot?" Lou asked.

"Could be guiding this whole thing."

"Interesting. Good thinking."

Once the celebration at the Kalamazoo station was over, the Missouri Four walked to their Lincoln on South Street. They had broken no laws so the police could not even detain them for questioning. The police decided to take extensive photos and to follow the vehicle.

The traffic was snarled in downtown Kalamazoo for about an hour after the event. As the jam dissipated, the Lincoln proceeded onto the campus of Western Michigan University. The driver pulled into the Athletic Department parking lot, taking a visitor's space. The four got out and went into the main office.

"May I help you gentlemen?" the receptionist asked.

"We're here to see Coach Avery."

"Is he expecting you?"

"Yes."

"Please have a seat in the waiting area. I'll page him."

A few minutes later, head football coach Buster Avery appeared and greeted the four men. "Welcome to Western Michigan University. Come on back to my office."

"Thank you," said Lance Lockwood, the spokesperson for the group. The other three seemed to be silent observers.

"I take it your trip up here was uneventful."

"Well, not exactly. Ted here has a lead foot. He thought he was on the Autobahn and we got pulled over by a state trooper."

"Did you get a ticket?"

"Billy, the comic, told the cop he was the Missouri Governor and that he had immunity. The cop bought it, warned us to slow down, and let us go!"

"Impersonating a governor, huh? There must be some law against that," Coach Avery remarked.

"There probably is, but it worked out for us," said Lance. "We were plenty early, and we heard about this Victory Ride event. Since none of us had ever seen a president, we decided to take it in."

"Yeah, the entire city has been really promoting the stop. President Southwell planned to announce a new college."

"He did," Lance replied. "Talk about a timely opportunity to put WMU on the map! The entire country was following the train on CNN, and when the President spoke, major networks interrupted programming to show him."

"Well, remind me again what brings the four of you to our campus?" Coach Avery asked.

"As I mentioned in my letter, we're visiting schools in the Mid-American Conference to convince them Central Missouri University would be a good fit in your conference."

"Oh yes, I recall now."

Billy spoke up. "Central Missouri is competitive in all of the major sports, and we have excellent facilities and a dedicated fan base. Also, we are fiscally solvent, as well as squeaky-clean, relative to the NCAA."

As the five men conversed, the Kalamazoo police reported to Lou the Lincoln's movements. The vehicle was registered to a Theodore Maglioto, at a Springfield, Missouri, address. The owner had no record with the law. Mr. Maglioto was an influential businessman in Springfield and a law-abiding citizen.

It finally became obvious to Lou that the Missouri Four had nothing to do with the Victory Ride, so he officially dismissed them from his list of suspects. Jack was right.

Needing to get to the bottom of the Shelly Westbrook drama, Lou called the Winnipeg Free Press. He didn't ask for the publisher or the editor, but for the editor's secretary, Amy Reder. Once he reached her, he began his questioning. "Hello, I'm Lou Searing, calling from Michigan. I am quite confused, and I'd like your help."

"I doubt I can help you," Amy replied. "I'm just a secretary/typist in the copy room."

"But, I think you are the one to help me," Lou persisted. "Do you know Shelly Westbrook?"

"Yes, I know Shell. We call her Shell around here. She is one of our correspondents, or reporters."

"She recently came to Winnipeg from Ottawa or Montreal?" Lou asked even though he knew the answer.

"Yes, she did."

"What was the reason for that?"

"I can only give you coffee-room chat."

"That's fine."

"Word is, she was demoted," Amy replied.

"And this was because?" Lou asked.

"I don't think I should say," Amy said, realizing she was talking to a stranger.

"Was it of a personal nature, like the Prime Minister has a mistress, or was it something of national importance, like classified information?" Lou continued to probe.

"We think it was something related to the RCMP and the Prime Minister."

"And that something might be...?" Lou continued.

"I don't think I should say any more."

"You do what you think is right, but a bit more information would be helpful," Lou begged. "Today a publicity event is going on in Michigan, the Victory Ride. The U.S. President, Michigan's Governor, and your Prime Minister began a train ride from Port Huron to New Buffalo to celebrate a high-speed rail contract. Early this morning the Governor received a threatening phone call, and in Lapeer your Prime Minister was wounded as he addressed the crowd. Then Shelly appeared in East Lansing, another stop on the tour. I am trying to understand: how 'Shell,' as you call her, ended up in East Lansing? That's the background. Now, is there anything else you can tell me?"

"I advise you to look into the VIA, and you should talk to the RCMP."

"The VIA?" Lou asked.

"Nobody knows for sure, but I've heard it's just a capitalized 'via,' you know, like 'by way of.'"

"Why is the RCMP involved?"

"They are responsible for the safety of the Prime Minister."

"Thank you for your help. May I have your name for my records?"

"No, and I hope you'll never mention this call. I could be fired, and who knows what else could happen to me," Amy said, finally realizing she should have kept quiet.

"I'll honor your request," Lou promised. "Thanks again."

As Lou hung up he thought, If this is a Canadian plot, and the Prime Minister is not on the train, there should be no more threat to the Victory Ride.

When Jack put 'Shelly Westbrook' into his Internet search engine on his laptop computer, hundreds of Internet sites filled his computer screen. Most of them were editorial material, focusing on the issue of French becoming Canada's national language. But one in particular caught Jack's eye. He clicked on the icon associated with the editorial and read:

HUGE MISTAKE BY THE PRIME MINISTER!
High-Speed Rail System to Focus on Toronto to Sarnia.

Prime Minister Leon Abernathy announced today that Canada will work with the United States to develop a high-speed rail system from Toronto to Sarnia. The U.S. will pick up the line in Port Huron and continue to Chicago on the Amtrak Blue Water Limited route. For this the Prime Minister should be SHOT (okay, a bit strong) or at least removed from office. Canada needs a high-speed rail system that goes at least from Quebec City to Vancouver (apologies to my friends in Nova Scotia).

The Prime Minister's plan is pure and simple payback to the citizens of southern Ontario, who voted heavily for the Prime Minister's party in the last election. This is one instance where the good of the nation as a whole should be foremost in the mind of our leader, as opposed to his personal interests and favors to the "folks back home."

Canadians everywhere must demand this traitor's resignation before further damage to the Republic is done. Readers will recall his statement that we should "start small" (Toronto to Sarnia) and learn from our mistakes before we tackle thousands of miles from the Atlantic to the Pacific. Starting small does nothing more than delay the progress we so desperately need in this 21st Century.

Stop this despot!!

—Shelly Westbrook, The Ottawa Gazette

Next, Jack pulled up the VIA web site, and typed "high-speed rail program" into the search space. Up popped a letter the president of VIA had sent to the Prime Minister. It read:

> *On behalf of the VIA Board of Directors, staff, and the employees of our VIA family serving Canadian citizens throughout the Provinces, I express unequivocally our disappointment in your support of a high-speed rail system for only a small fraction of the country. The VIA Board is frustrated by the lack of vision of our government leader. The decision to work with the United States, instead of forging ahead with the assistance of our European and Japanese friends, is totally alarming.*
>
> *The VIA Board, its thousands of employees, and millions of riders urge you to reverse this course of action before it's too late. This plan is not good policy for Canada, and we implore you to work with us in developing the world's finest rail system.*
>
> *Sincerely,*
> *Edward Stevens, President and CEO of VIA*

Jack showed the letter to Lou who read it with much interest. "I know there is strong emotion surrounding this initiative, but every decision made by a politician favors someone and disfavors another. I can't accept that Canadians would plot to kill their Prime Minister over this. Am I off-base, Jack?"

"I see your point, but it's an emotional issue that seems fraught with disaster in the eyes of some. It doesn't take much for a few people with loose screws to take matters into their own hands."

"You know what's becoming clear to me now, Jack?"

"What's on your mind, Lou?"

"It makes sense that someone—or a small group—knows about this conflict between the Prime Minister and the VIA. This person or group sees a wonderful opportunity to cause an international crisis, including the death of officials, knowing that the blame will certainly be cast upon those who are obviously upset. I'm referring to Shelly Westbrook and the VIA Board."

"That makes sense, but who in the U.S. would want to harm the Prime Minister?" Jack asked.

"You've got me on that one."

CHAPTER FOURTEEN

The stop in Dowagiac was intended to be brief and indeed it was. The only thing that stood out was the variety of protest signs in the crowd. The Tea Party was dominant. The President and Governor viewed signs that read, "Too Much Government!" "Invest in a HORSE, not a Train," and "Big Government Get Off Our Backs!" The stop was, by far, the coolest reception the Victory Ride had received. There were no bands and only a few hundred gathered. The politicians were even booed, to the surprise of many.

Citizens took advantage of the opportunity to let Governor Halloran know how they felt about his budget and the rise in taxes needed to balance same. Needless to say, everyone on board was eager for the train to head south to Niles.

Once again, the Victory Ride stopped about a mile from its destination so the local dignitaries—Mayor Marty Erickson and Father McGinney, President of the University of Notre Dame—could get on.

Niles was approaching its celebration differently. Much to the relief of security, the Niles officials chose to hold the celebration in the high school auditorium. The number of people would be limited, but security would be assured. And, it would give the folks on the train a chance to walk on terra firma, for the ride had been underway since the early hours of the morning.

The train would pull up to the station, where a crowd was anticipated. Everyone hoped to catch a glimpse of the President moving between the train and his personal vehicle. The band was already in the high school auditorium. Because security was assured, there was no need for the Plexiglas shield in front of the speakers. The Secret Service had approved the entire high school staff, the band, and dignitaries who would be attending. All of the paperwork had been sent to Washington, D.C. weeks before.

When the President's security staff entered the building, more than one glanced at the custodian watching from a doorway. Something about him caused the President's people to contact the Principal and Superintendent of Niles Public Schools to inquire about the man.

They learned that he was a parolee who had been given a chance to redeem himself. He had been an accomplice to a robbery, and he was deemed no threat to anyone. The security team accepted the explanation but remained concerned because the man seemed most anxious, quickly looking back and forth.

The VIPs entered through the side door of the high school and were directed backstage where a short gathering addressed the order of speaking and time constraints. The Notre Dame President, Father McGinney, would be recognized, but would not speak because his remarks were not cleared in advance.

The audience was anxious for the celebration to begin. The train had arrived almost three hours late, and people were getting hungry and edgy; someone started rhythmic clapping to show their disappointment in the long wait. The janitor walked out on the stage, checked out the microphone, and placed a glass of water on the podium.

No one thought anything of the janitor's action except Cindy Bell, who was president of the Honor Society. Cindy was fascinated by investigations and forensic science. She saw this visit as an opportunity to observe protocols and procedures to be followed in case of security breach. Cindy wondered, *Was that water approved as it came from its source? Was it from a faucet or was it from a sealed bottle? Was it checked in some way before the janitor took it to the podium?* She could only assume that it was safe, but certainly, it remained a point of curiosity.

The rhythmic clapping continued until the curtain opened. Standing side by side on the stage were the Niles mayor, the Governor, the President of the United States, and the President of Notre Dame.

While each dignitary offered comments and all networks carried the event live, a member of the RCMP escorted Shelly to the airport's conference room. She understood the Prime Minister wanted to see her, and that the meeting would be brief. She walked into the conference room with a security guard holding her arm. He invited her to sit in a chair and offered to get her some water.

Shortly thereafter Prime Minister Abernathy entered the room, took his seat and opened a bottle of water. "You wanted to see me," Shelly said cautiously.

"Yes. I do. In fact, I directed my flight here only to have a chance to talk with you."

"But you could have called," Shelly replied.

"I realize that, but I wanted to talk with you privately." The Prime Minister asked the security team to go out of the conference room for a moment. Shelly felt she might have an anxiety attack not knowing what would be said or done.

"Here is some paper, a pen, and a small recorder. I want you to do a story to go onto the wire this evening and to appear in tomorrow's Winnipeg Free Press."

"I don't have control over that," Shelly replied. "My publisher makes those decisions, and he usually consults my editor first."

"I appreciate protocol, and I don't have a problem with you going through channels. In fact, I would expect it."

"What shall I write?" Shelly asked.

"A story about the power of the press and of the people of Canada. I want you to tell them that I sought you out to tell this story. I have listened to the people, reconsidered, and decided to support a high-speed rail system to traverse our great country. However, I will also concurrently support the small project between Toronto and Sarnia, as I said I would. There will be no delay; construction on our long-distance rail system will commence at the same time the Ontario project begins."

"I must say that I'm pleasantly surprised at this—shocked actually," Shelly responded.

"Yes, I imagine you are."

"Are you giving in to political pressure?" Shelly asked.

"No. I simply took time on the Victory Ride to think about Canada and our need for this high-speed system. I'm going to ask you not to print what I am about to say. I am truly sorry about your arrest this morning. I authorized it out of fear that you or someone with you would literally blow up the train. I should not have assumed this, and I am sorry."

"I accept your apology," Shelly said humbly. "Thank you."

"You're welcome."

"I guess I had better get to work on this story. It's big news for Canada, and for you, sir. You may become known as the Father of Rail Transportation in the 21st Century. Thank you for allowing me to break the news."

"I did it because I admire you. You always state your thoughts clearly and in a manner that resonates with your readers."

"Thank you, Mr. Prime Minister."

Just as the two were about to rise and part company, the door to the conference room opened and in walked Major Buzz Houchins of the RCMP. "Excuse me, Mr. Prime Minister. It's common knowledge that your ears are quite painful on flights. I use this gum on my flights and I find it most effective. I thought you might like some comfort on your long flight to Ottawa after a most tiring day."

"Thank you, Buzz. This is appreciated."

As Major Houchins turned to leave, Shelly rose, shook the Prime Minister's outstretched hand, turned, and walked out of the airport to a car provided by her editor. The Prime Minister and his entourage got back on the plane, and within minutes the plane lifted off for a long flight east. After a long day, the Prime Minister chewed his gum, put his head back on the pillow, relaxed for the first time since early morning, and fell asleep.

Cindy Bell kept an eye on the glass of water. When the mayor spoke, she noticed that he did not take a drink. When the Governor spoke, he did not drink. The President spoke, but he turned to an aide who handed him a plastic container, ignoring the water on the podium.

Father McGinney, who was not authorized to speak, asked if he might say a few words. The mayor nodded curtly, a less-than-pleased look in his eye. Father McGinney stepped to the podium and said, "I realize that I am a guest here this evening, but I want to offer my congratulations to the State of Michigan and the Province of Ontario for winning this high-speed rail project. It will be exciting to watch Michigan embrace this new technology and advance it throughout the country."

He appeared to have a catch in his throat, coughed quietly a couple of times, and then took a drink from the glass on the podium. He then said, "God's blessings on all of you," and stepped back, standing quietly while the mayor thanked the people for participating in an event that would go into the history books for Niles, Michigan.

The entourage was escorted back to the train under tight security. With hardly a soul in the vicinity, President Fortner, Father McGinney, and Governor Halloran stepped up and made themselves comfortable in the private car. Governor Halloran tended to some phone calls and messages from aides and his secretary. President Fortner had no more than said, "Remind me again what the focus of our discussion is going to be on our way to the next stop..." when Father McGinney fell out of his seat and into the aisle of the train. He was immediately helped to the medical car and hoisted onto a gurney. The President's personal physician, Dr. Spoelman, discovered rapid heartbeat, intense nausea, and profuse sweating.

"I suspect a heart attack, but I don't have the proper medical equipment on board to treat this man if surgery is needed," Dr. Spoelman explained to the President. "We've got to get him to a trauma center—fast!"

As the train waited for an ambulance at the next crossing the Notre Dame President seemed to steadily improve. His aide was not surprised. "This has happened before. It has been a very stressful day for Father. His calendar has been full and he's been in some very stressful meetings. I think if you just monitor his vitals, we'll go to the Pawating Hospital in Niles, run some tests, and get him back on his feet."

A presidential aide reported that a student at the high school had said that the janitor brought out the glass of water. She noted that only Father drank from the glass, and perhaps the water was poisoned. He added, "I thanked her for her keen observation. However, there's nothing to worry about; I approved the glass of water on the podium. In fact, I asked the janitor to put it on the podium. It was my understanding that Father McGinney always wants a glass of water handy, even if he is not going to say much."

By the time the ambulance arrived at the crossing, Father was sitting up and his color was coming back, but he appeared very weak. However, he was talking to his aide and the President's personal physician, which they all took as positive signs.

Once Shelly Westbrook was back at the Winnipeg Free Press, she immediately walked to her editor's office. "Wait till you hear this!" she exclaimed.

"Calm down, calm down. Does the boss need to hear this?" Susan Northrup asked.

"Yes, it could very well be his biggest scoop."

"Let me call him in," Susan replied. "No sense in you giving the news twice."

The publisher answered his pager and came immediately to the editor's office. "Someone has a scoop?" he asked.

"OK, Shelly, go ahead," Susan said.

"The Prime Minister told me personally that he is going to support a speed-rail route across Canada. He has reconsidered the decision to go with just a short route through Ontario, and he thinks having our own route from coast to coast is a better policy decision. He credited me and my writing for helping to change his opinion on the matter."

"Wow, that is news," the publisher said with a smile. "We've got the scoop—and ahead of Ottawa, Toronto, Calgary, and Vancouver. There might be a Pulitzer in this for you, Shelly."

"So, I go with it?" Shelly asked. "I can get copy to you in a matter of minutes."

"I can't imagine a bigger story for the Free Press," Susan said.

"He wanted me to put the story on the wire."

"Fine with me, as long as the Winnipeg Free Press and you get credit for breaking the news in Canada."

The publisher left smiling; Susan remarked, "That's the first time in years I've seen a smile on Ken Workman's face. You made his day, Shelly! There may be a raise in this for you."

"Thanks, but with all due respect, I'd rather be forgiven my sins and move back to Ottawa."

"That just might happen," Susan said. "Tell me, Shelly, how could the assassin miss the Prime Minister this morning?"

"I haven't a clue."

"I guess in retrospect, in view of recent events, it was good that he missed."

The EMS crew was able to get Father McGinney off the Victory Ride and into the ambulance. The train continued west to New Buffalo and the ambulance went east to Niles.

New Buffalo, the last stop, was about a half-hour away. It was early evening, and most who had come out for the celebration when it was scheduled for late afternoon had left. Some said they'd come back, but many had evening plans. The high school band had been dismissed once it was determined the train would be so late. The Berrien County political party representatives even wondered whether staying, or coming back for that matter, might not be worth their time and energy. The network media were on hand and would be the last to leave. They had a lot of experience waiting for events to start or for dignitaries to appear.

The Governor and President were adamant about holding the ceremony, even if only a few people turned out.

Actually, more than a few people came to stand by the platform. And the closer to the train's arrival, the more people came. The event began to take on a festive air. A local bagpiper band sent up a lot of hot air for entertainment. Their kilts were colorful, and—since the tunes were recognizable—the music was tolerable.

Five-year-old twins appeared, each holding a large bouquet of roses; one for the Governor, and the other for the President. People with signs gathered for blocks around the Amtrak station. Signs read, "We may be the last stop, but we are the BEST stop!" And "Thank you, Mr. President, for helping the people of Michigan."

Also on hand were the mayors of Michigan City, Indiana, and Chicago, Illinois. The train would eventually cross the northwest corner of Indiana and into Illinois up to Chicago. The Victory Ride would end in New Buffalo, but when built, the train would continue through Indiana to Chicago.

As more and more people arrived at the Amtrak station, more law enforcement officers appeared. The crowd was as orderly as people can be while anticipating the arrival of the President of the United States.

On a lark, Jack tried to call Shelly Westbrook on his cell. To his amazement, she picked up. "Hello."

"Shelly, this is Jack Kelly in Michigan."

"Oh, hi, Jack. Crazy day, huh?"

"You can say that again. What happened after the state trooper took you away in his cruiser?"

"We went to an airport outside of Clare, and then I flew to Winnipeg. You're not going to believe what happened next."

"Try me."

"Someone in law enforcement met my plane. I was escorted to the airport conference room. The Prime Minister appeared and said he had changed his mind about the high-speed rail service in Canada. He now supports a transcontinental system."

"That's a switch in policy."

"Big-time, Jack. Is the Victory Ride over yet?" Shelly asked.

"One more stop—New Buffalo. We still haven't solved the day's mysteries."

"Very complex, Jack."

"It is, but when Lou gets his teeth into these cases, he doesn't let go until the whole thing is solved."

"One good thing is, no one has died," Shelly said.

"Not yet, anyway, and we've got our fingers crossed that an hour from now we can say the same thing."

"Well, if it helps, I'll cross my fingers too."

"I'm glad you're safely in Winnipeg and have a big story for the morning edition."

"Jack. I've an explanation for much of what happened today, but I can't tell you all of it."

"I see." Jack pulled out his notebook and pen.

"For now, be advised that an assassin may be up on the water tower across from the station in New Buffalo. His name is Les Trousard."

"Sounds like an obvious position. Wouldn't security arrest him?" Jack asked.

"Not if he's wearing a police uniform."

"So, that's the big event planned for the Victory Ride. It won't be much of a victory; Michigan receives a multi-billion dollar opportunity, and a president is killed."

"You got it."

"Thanks for this tip. But, had I not called, you wouldn't have told me this, or were you going to call me or Lou?"

"I guess some things are meant to be," Shelly replied.

"Naturally, I'm curious how you know this. Are you part of a conspiracy? You probably were part of it while you were in East Lansing."

"I can't talk about it now, Jack. Go and save the life of your President. You'll be famous forever—and it couldn't happen to a nicer guy. Your thanks to me will be to say nothing about how you know the location of the shooter, or even that there will be a shooter."

"My lips are sealed, and I don't talk in my sleep. Or so Elaine tells me."

"Got to run, Jack."

"Thanks. Watch the news."

Jack told Lou what he knew. When Lou heard Jack's news, he didn't hesitate. He went immediately to the President and the head of the Secret Service.

"We've received a tip about a threat to the President's life. We'll do what we can to help, which is to get out of the way of you professionals." He then explained what Jack had learned.

Immediately word was sent to be on the lookout for an assassin on the water tower or anyone on the ground with a package which could hold a rifle. Officers were directed to take no action, but to report to the Secret Service if someone appeared suspicious. While it obviously wasn't planned, the story was leaked, and the media learned of the possible assassin in New Buffalo.

"Mr. President, we'll keep you informed," Marcia Ludlow said. "Right now you are to go to the media car. It's the last place an assassin would look for the President." President Fortner rose from his office seat on the train and made his way to the media car.

CHAPTER FIFTEEN

A man dressed in a blue police uniform calmly walked into the crowd. He was carrying a rifle and appeared to be a part of a community force to assist in security. He walked up to an officer and asked, "Who's in charge here? I need to get my orders."

"The man standing next to the squad car by that CBS trailer is the Chief."

"Thanks."

The officer in blue walked over to the chief and introduced himself. "My chief told me to report to you, to see what I could do to help."

"Good. We can't have enough security around here this evening. Stand on the second step of the platform. Face the crowd and be on the lookout for anyone acting suspicious."

"Yes, sir." The officer walked away quickly because the chief had others waiting to talk with him.

What Lou and Jack couldn't figure out was how Shelly knew about the assassin. "She has to be a part of the conspiracy," Lou insisted.

"I agree," Jack replied. "How else could she know the guy's name, and that there is going to be an attempt to assassinate the President in New Buffalo?"

"If we can avert the attempt on the President's life, we can put the Victory Ride to bed. Then we can work on solving the other mysteries."

"Right," Jack agreed. "And so far, the person with the key to the mysteries is Shelly Westbrook."

"Of course, it's possible that Shelly is not a part of the conspiracy, but is only knowledgeable about the plan to wreak havoc on Michigan."

"I think we should leave protection of the President to the Secret Service. There's really nothing we can do, it seems to me," Jack summarized.

"I need to talk to Shelly," Lou said as he dialed her number.

"Hello, Mr. Searing," Shelly answered.

"Thank you for talking with Jack," Lou began. "You have helped prevent a tragedy and we will keep Jack's word to you that we will try not to divulge our source. But I can't assure you I'll not be subpoenaed to testify."

"Thank you. I understand."

"But, Shelly, certainly you know about this strange series of events as the Ride crossed Michigan. What else can you tell me to explain them?"

"I am willing to help you stop the assassination of your President, but that's as far as I can go."

"I respect that. But if Jack hadn't called to see how you were, you wouldn't have told him about the planned assassination. This seems a terrible load on your conscience. To have a man die, and to have known about it and not taken steps to prevent a crime of historic proportions would be hard to live with."

There was a telling pause before Shelly replied. "I don't know what to say."

Lou's voice became hard as he got to the point. "Are you part of a conspiracy behind the disruptions on today's Victory Ride?"

Shelly hesitated, then sighed deeply. "Yes."

"Why, Shelly? What is the conspiracy meant to accomplish? Are only a few in on this, or is it the action of a large group?"

"It started as a love triangle. It's a few people who were incensed when the Prime Minister and the President endorsed the high-speed rail system in southern Ontario and Michigan. We thought we could use violence to change or stop the plan."

"And risk life in prison? You folks sure must have believed you could pull this off."

"Yes, we did. And, we believed a new Prime Minister would not approve a short route, but one stretching across Canada."

"You said, 'A new Prime Minister,'" Lou replied. "Does that mean a potential Prime Minister was part of the conspiracy?"

"No, absolutely not!" Shelly replied quickly and firmly.

"Assuming the Ride ends peacefully—and since the Prime Minister has changed his mind—can I assume that there is no more conspiracy?"

"Well…"

"According to you, there is an assassin in New Buffalo waiting to kill the President. Why? Why do the conspirators care what happens, now that your Prime Minister has changed his mind and you'll get your way?"

"I see your point."

"If I were you, I would contact this assassin and call it off," Lou advised. "I can assure you that if someone shoots our President, and even if he misses, you'll be writing for the prison paper. Is it really worth it? If you are a sane and compassionate soul, you have to intervene."

"I don't have any way to reach him, Lou."

"I just don't get it, Shelly. I will protect you to the extent I can. If you wish to give me more information or if I can help, let me know, OK?"

"OK."

As the Victory Ride rattled along to New Buffalo, Lou asked to speak with the head of the Secret Service. Both the agent and the President appeared. "You wanted to see me?" the agent said.

Lou looked directly at President Fortner. "I have reason to believe that there will be an attempt to kill you in New Buffalo, Mr. President. I am not sure exactly how the attempt will be carried out, but I believe it is to be by rifle shot." Lou turned to the agent and continued, "I imagine you have options available when faced with this kind of threat."

"Yes," replied the agent. "First of all, thank you. Second, it's up to the President if he wishes to step out onto the platform to address the crowd. He, too, has some options. He can wear a security outfit…"

"Excuse me, what's that?" Lou asked.

"It's made of a flexible material that will retard penetration by a rifle bullet."

"Really. I'd heard of a bullet-proof vest, but not a whole security outfit."

"He wears it under his suit, like long underwear, in addition to the traditional bullet-proof vest," the head of Secret Service explained.

"What protection is there for the head?"

"He can wear a scarf high on his neck and a wide-brimmed hat also made of the same material."

"I see."

"Or, we have a look-alike on board who could wear the same protective garments."

"I don't like to use the decoy, because I think the American people deserve to see me," the President stated with authority. "But, if the threat is real, it is an option."

"Or as you said earlier, you could stay on the train," Lou reminded the two.

"Yes, but I didn't come from D.C. to spend my time hiding in a railroad car," remarked the President.

"I understand."

The Victory Ride pulled into New Buffalo to a boisterous crowd, thankful that history had come to their small town. The local high school band, who had appeared when a chain call summoned everyone back to the event, entertained the crowd, while final plans for speaking were being made inside the train. The mayor of New Buffalo would speak first, followed by the Governor, and finally the President.

The crowd numbered in the thousands, all coming to see the President. The man in the East Lansing officer uniform took his place on the second step at the side of the platform. He couldn't have wished for a better position for a shot to kill the President.

Two other officers walked together throughout the crowd, their eyes searching left and right for anything suspicious. One said to the other, "Isn't an East Lansing officer a bit out of place down here?"

"Yes, but my guess is the chief put out a call for police departments to send anyone they could spare."

"I understand, but only one officer?"

"Maybe he has relatives here and was coming anyway. Or, maybe he has a cottage in the area and could come over with little effort."

"I suppose so, but I still think it's strange."

"Check on it then. It's our job to report anything suspicious."

The officer called the chief. "Yes, I know about him. No problem. He sought me out and wanted to know how he could help. I'm okay with it."

The officer was still convinced that this wasn't normal. As he walked along the train, he caught Jack's attention; he'd been looking out the window at the ever-increasing crowd. Jack's eyes constantly scanned the scene, but he saw nothing out of the ordinary. The officer signaled to Jack that he wanted to talk with him.

Jack emerged from the media car and approached the officer. "You wanted to talk to me?"

"Yes, see that officer on the second step of the platform?"

Jack nodded. "Yes."

"He's supposedly from East Lansing. He says his chief told him to come here to help with security."

"Uh-huh."

"Possible, but if you looked at the officers here, they're all from local communities—St. Joseph, Benton Harbor, Niles, Berrien Springs—not one officer is from outside of Berrien County. But that guy approached our chief and said he was sent down by his chief to help."

"Thanks."

Jack walked to the edge of the crowd and used his cell to call Evan Fleming, Chief of Police in East Lansing.

"Did you authorize an officer from East Lansing to assist security on the Victory Ride in New Buffalo?" Jack asked.

"I'll help any chief who asks for it," Chief Fleming replied. "But I wasn't asked, and no, I didn't send anyone down there."

Then it hit Jack. The officer who had been Tasered behind the train at the East Lansing station was stripped of his uniform and his rifle stolen. That has to be the assassin! Jack thought.

Lou answered his phone as the Mayor was making his remarks. "Yes, Jack."

"The officer on the second step of the platform—left side as you look to the crowd. He's in an East Lansing uniform and has a rifle. The East Lansing chief didn't send an officer here.

Remember the officer who was Tasered and had his rifle and uniform stolen?"

"Sure do."

"I think that guy took the uniform and rifle and now is about to kill the President."

"Thanks, Jack."

Lou quickly alerted the head of Secret Service to the officer on the second step of the platform. The Governor was beginning to introduce the President when two Secret Service officers came out of the train. They immediately went down the steps, and before the gunman could whirl to fire, they disarmed him and wrestled him to the ground as other officers came to their aid.

The media was all over the activity. The crowd wasn't sure what was going on, but they knew something important had happened, and rumors spread quickly.

The Governor, still at the microphone, tried to regain order. "Attention please! Ladies and gentlemen, please give me your attention!" The crowd quieted a bit as the gunman was whisked out of sight.

The Governor continued. "Please remain calm and I will explain." Finally the crowd stopped jostling. "We received a threat on the life of the President, and we took action to remove that threat. We feel it is now safe to proceed. Please give a big New Buffalo welcome to your President, Alan Fortner!"

The President came out of the train car and approached the microphone. "Thank you! Thank you! I apologize for the disruption but we must be constantly vigilant for persons who aim to disrupt our freedoms. Fortunately, as a result of fast action of the New Buffalo police and my Secret Service, we were able to avoid a major crisis."

The audience clapped wildly. "Again, thank you for coming out to greet the Victory Ride. We began in Port Huron early this morning, and it's been a long day, as you can imagine. The Prime Minister of Canada was wounded, and he was treated on the train. However, the threat was credible enough that he thought it prudent to leave us.

"Your Governor was adamant that we continue. This is a special day for Michigan because the high-speed rail service project will bring jobs. Michigan will turn around by leading the nation in a new technology. When we stopped in Kalamazoo just a few hours ago, President Southwell of Western Michigan University informed us that he will establish a College of Transportation to provide the skills needed for this century and beyond."

Again, the audience roared in approval and appreciation.

"But now it's time to end the Victory Ride here with the citizens of Berrien County—home of the Fruit Festival, sandy beaches, and friendly people. Thanks again for your hospitality. Good-bye."

The President waved, turned, and walked back into the train car, and the crowd slowly dispersed. Shortly, the presidential limousine pulled up, threading its way through a host of cars and vans loading up media equipment.

The limo left New Buffalo and made its way to the South Bend airport, where Air Force One waited for a tired President. The networks had their correspondents and microphones on the scene in case the President was willing to speak; they broke into regular programming as the President walked to a bank of microphones at the base of the steps leading into the plane.

"I have just come from an all-day journey across the Great Lake State of Michigan. Michigan's Governor, Roland Halloran hosted a Victory Ride to celebrate the high-speed rail project awarded to Michigan by Congress. My colleague and friend, the Prime Minister of Canada, joined us because the eastern point of this project is Toronto, Canada. And, so the Prime Minister, the Governor of Michigan, and the mayors of cities along the proposed route met wonderful people who came out to celebrate Michigan becoming the center of a new industry in the United States and in North America.

"Unfortunately, there were some negative aspects to the trip, as well. Prime Minister Abernathy was wounded by a gunman, who remains on the run. We have committed our law enforcement officers to assist Canada in apprehending the person or persons responsible for this crime on United States soil. Local police and my security team were instrumental in neutralizing another threat before I was in any danger. And, I must give special recognition to two citizens who worked behind the scenes to assure our safety. I refer to Lou Searing of Grand Haven and his assistant, Jack Kelly, of Muskegon.

"I look forward to being back in the White House in a few hours. It has been a most satisfying day, in spite of the danger and the unfortunate events. I regret I don't have time for questions. Please contact my press secretary for any clarifications you need. Thank you."

With that, he turned and walked up the steps of Air Force One and the door closed behind him. The plane was cleared for takeoff and was soon on its way to Washington, D.C.

CHAPTER SIXTEEN

A media person was heard to say, "A lot of public exposure with no deaths and one injury. The Michigan crowds were respectful, law abiding, and controlled."

While Lou and Jack were thankful for a peaceful end to the Victory Ride, there remained the mystery of the conspiracy and investigations of criminal acts.

The would-be assassin, disguised as a police officer, was Les Trousard, a former marksman and a former member of the Royal Canadian Mounted Police. Once identified, Les went silently, awaiting an attorney. Because he was a suspect in a conspiracy to harm the President, the FBI had jurisdiction.

The head of the FBI, Robert Singleton, authorized Lou and Jack to work with the Detroit Office to resolve the matter. The Canadian government asked the United States to turn the suspect over for prosecution in the assassination attempt on the Prime Minister, but the United States, with all due respect, declined to grant the request. Les would remain in the United States awaiting prosecution for the threat on the President's life, the Prime Minister's life, and the attack on the East Lansing police officer.

Lou deliberately did not inform the FBI of the source of the information which led to saving the President's life. Lou and Jack now knew that it had been a conspiracy at work and not the desire of one person to wreak havoc on U.S. soil.

They were aware of two conspirators—Shelly Westbrook and Les Trousard—but who else might have been involved?

Unknown to Lou and Jack, Shelly Westbrook—although not under arrest—was being questioned by the Royal Canadian Mounted Police. The RCMP had studied video from the East Lansing stop of the Victory Ride and easily picked out Shelly in a crowd photo.

A detective with the RCMP asked, "Why were you in Michigan, specifically East Lansing, when the Victory Ride stopped for an event?"

"I was doing a story about our government's response to possible terrorism. My newspaper got permission for me to fly as a guest on a Canadian Air Force scramble to Toronto, to give legitimacy to my story. The pilot of the aircraft was ordered to land in Lansing because the Prime Minister had been shot and there was concern that this was the beginning of a terrorist strike. We didn't know how long the plane would be grounded, so I went to the Lansing newspaper office to check the wire for news.

"While there, I learned about the Victory Ride, and since I was literally only five miles from the train station, I asked to be taken there."

The detective continued his questioning. "You realized that you might miss your flight if the mission was to resume?"

"I suppose, but my journalistic nose followed the story and I assumed that risk. While I was covering the East Lansing stop, the Prime Minister saw me in the crowd and had me arrested."

"But you escaped."

"I wouldn't say 'escaped,' but the arresting officer somehow passed out. I called for help, and while the attention was on him, I walked away."

"And then?" the detective asked.

"I called my editor with my dilemma. My newspaper made arrangements to get me home."

"Were you involved with others in a plan to kill the Prime Minister?" the detective asked outright.

"Of course not! I might be a burr under the government's saddle, and my opinion pieces show my dislike of the Prime Minister's policies and practices, but no, I would not be so stupid as to risk life in prison for such a hideous crime."

"Do you know of a conspiracy to kill the Prime Minister and/or the President of the United States?"

"I suspect there was a conspiracy," Shelly replied after a telling pause. "I imagine that the suspect you have in custody, Les Trousard, is a marksman, but I suspect he was not the one to propose the shooting. I believe he was contracted to kill."

"I see," the detective replied. "Do you have any idea who might be behind the plan to kill these national leaders?"

"I don't have any names, but I was fed information for my articles by a group of Canadians who are furious with our government and the United States for awarding the high-speed rail project to Michigan. Our Prime Minister supported only a small section of southern Ontario for the Canadian High-Speed rail initiative."

"Do you have a contact within this group?" the detective continued.

"No, communication was a one-way street—they sent me information. I never contacted them, nor did I ever meet with anyone."

"So, when you say you suspect there was a conspiracy, you are suggesting this informal group is involved."

"That's logical."

"Do you know Les Trousard?"

"Only through information that came to me, as I already mentioned."

"Did anyone tell you outright that there would be an attempt on the life of the Prime Minister?"

"No. But, later in the day I heard about Les and a plan to kill the U.S. President."

"What did you do with this information?"

"Suffice it to say that I alerted security on the Victory Ride."

"So, it was your warning that saved the President's life?"

"That appears to be the case."

Jack began to research Les Trousard, and the Internet yielded considerable information. His Facebook page contained a lot of clues. He had written the previous day: "Going to see my Uncle Sam. They're calling the family together. The old man is about to pass on."

Jack thought, *If he has an uncle Sam, this could be legit, but I'm fairly certain he is talking about the U.S. Government, and Uncle Sam could be a code phrase for the Prime Minister.*

He then noticed a response from Shelly Westbrook. "Les, listen to me. This isn't worth murder. I've reconsidered the consequences. Stay home!! If you must do something, only wound the Prime Minister."

Jack thought, These people are crazy for putting this on the Internet. Surely they're smart enough to realize that this could be found and would be enough to put them in the slammer for the rest of their lives. Shelly could say she tried to get Les to stop, but the post places her within the conspiracy.

Jack looked at earlier messages from Shelly, "Major Houchins will direct a pilot to go on a scramble training mission, tell him to land in Lansing ahead of the Victory Ride. The pilot will take me under the pretext of a story on the Air Force's ability to respond to a terrorist attack."

When Jack shared what he had found with Lou, he called Shelly. "Good evening, Shelly."

"Hello, Mr. Searing. Thank you for intervening to save the life of your President."

"Thank you for the information that allowed us to do so."

"You're welcome."

"I'm calling to help you. The authorities have identified Les as the gunman who threatened the life of the President. He has an attorney and so far has not said a word. Jack dug up what he could about Les on the Internet. His Facebook page contains exchanges that implicate the two of you, enough to have you arrested for conspiracy, though you might get some points for trying to convince Les to not carry out the plan."

"On his Facebook page?" Shelly asked nervously. "That can't be."

"I'm not playing games, Shelly. If you don't believe me, go to his page and see for yourself."

"I have no reason to doubt you. You said you were calling to help me," Shelly reminded Lou.

"Who is this Major Houchins, Shelly?"

"How did you learn of him?"

"My source is confidential. Who is he?" Lou persisted.

"He's the one behind the assassination attempt on the Prime Minister."

"You said this plot started as a love triangle. Is this where Houchins comes in?" Lou asked. There was a long pause. Lou continued. "Listen Shelly. You are in this deep, very deep. You can help yourself by explaining what happened."

"Okay. The love triangle was Buzz, Leon, and Norma, Buzz's wife. Leon and Norma were having an affair many years ago. It lasted about a year. Leon went into politics and Buzz worked his way up in the Royal Canadian Mounted Police. Buzz hated Leon since the moment he learned of the affair and vowed to kill him."

"How does Les figure into all of this?" Lou asked.

"Les and Randal were saved by Houchins following a boating accident north of Winnipeg. Les told Buzz that he would do whatever he asked as a thank you for saving them from death by drowning."

"Pay back," Lou replied.

"Exactly."

"So why was the speed-rail decision the straw that broke the camel's back?" Lou asked.

"Because Buzz's brother stood to make millions, if not billions of dollars if the speed rail system went coast to coast and he wasn't getting any younger."

"So, we get revenge for an affair and a new supportive Prime Minister by asking a marksman to follow through on a promise made in a warm lodge in northern Manitoba," Lou concluded.

"Yes, that's the story, except the marksman was insane," Shelly confessed.

"Why do you come into the picture?" Lou asked.

"Because Buzz knew my feelings aligned with his brother's and he knew we both hated the Prime Minister. He asked me to help plan it and, of course, I would have the lead story when the assassination occurred."

"So, you come up with a story idea and request going on the flight on the day of the Victory Ride. Les was to kill the Prime Minister in Lapeer, or—if not successful—to kill him in East Lansing. On his own he decides to kill the President of the United States to protect himself from Buzz's revenge."

"Yes. Now you've got it," Shelly said. "But there is more. Tomorrow you will hear that Buzz committed suicide late this afternoon. You will find that he left no note, and friends and family are shocked and will have no explanation for his action."

"I have a question for you," Lou said.

"Go ahead."

"Is this it? The conspiracy was the four of you, and no one else was involved or knows anything about this. Am I correct?"

For a few seconds there was silence on the other end. Then Lou thought he heard a commotion, but with his hearing loss, he couldn't be sure. However, Shelly was no longer on the line. Lou listened for a few seconds before finally breaking the connection.

Lou turned to Jack. "We've gotten ourselves into one heck of an ethical mess."

"How's that?"

"I can't tell you. If I do, you will be privy to information that I don't want you to have for your own safety. Just trust me. It's information that only two other people have."

"Does it explain the mystery?" Jack asked, seeking closure. "Is the case solved?"

"I can't say. Excuse me," Lou walked away with head down, deep in thought. *Can I trust Shelly Westbrook? Did this Houchins commit suicide, or did Shelly kill him to keep him quiet?*

Lou called the FBI. "Agent Hilgar," a voice answered.

"This is Lou Searing."

"Yes, Mr. Searing. How can we help you?"

"I need to know where you are keeping Les Trousard."

"Right now he's in the Berrien County Jail."

"Is he on a suicide watch?"

"Not at the moment—should he be?" Agent Hilgar asked.

"I'd recommend it, yes," Lou replied. "I have good reason to make this request."

"I'll arrange for it."

"I'd also like to visit the jail. I want to talk with Les and his attorney, just the three of us, no video recording, no others in the room."

"His attorney is talking with him right now. Where are you? I'll get transportation for you."

"I'm at Oinks Dutch Treat, an ice cream place here in New Buffalo.

"We're on our way. Should only take 10 minutes or so to get there. Is Jack coming along?"

"Yes, but I alone will be talking with Les and his attorney."

While waiting for the ride to St. Joseph, Lou called Carol. "What a day!" he sighed.

"There's an understatement if I ever heard one," Carol replied. "I've been watching CNN for most of the day. In fact, I've seen you more on television today than I might normally see you at home. And, the President praised you and Jack by name. Is that cool, or what?"

"It's been a day full of confusion, drama, anticipation, close calls. I feel like Indiana Jones."

"I can imagine. But, I didn't see a whip over your shoulder."

"The only whip I carried was my mind, and I used it often."

"Are you coming home soon?" Carol asked, hoping for a positive response.

"I'd like to. Our cars are in Flint and Durand—at least, I think that's where they are. I've been in so many places today; I forget what we rented and where they've been left."

"Want me to come down and get you?" Carol asked.

"That would be great, if you don't mind."

"Where are you? I have my cell, so I'll be in touch as I get closer. It could be almost an hour before I get there."

"I'm in New Buffalo now, at a really neat ice cream place."

"Why am I not surprised?" Carol asked, knowing if ice cream were in the area, Lou would find it.

"You know me—got to have my Mackinaw Island Fudge, Moose Tracks or something like that."

"Enjoy it, Lou," Carol said sincerely. "It's been a long day for you."

"I will. We'll be leaving soon for St. Joseph and the Berrien County Jail."

"Okay. I'm on my way," Carol said. "We're going to be late getting home."

"We ought to be home around midnight. Obviously Jack will be coming with us. Please call Elaine and let her know what the plan is. I think Jack will call her too, if he hasn't already."

"Okay. See you soon. Get something to eat and relax a bit."

"I will."

Jack and Lou were about finished eating their ice cream cones when a sheriff's car pulled up outside Oink's Dutch Treat.

"Come on, Jack—we're off to St. Joe."

When Lou and Jack got to the county jail, Lou was ushered into a conference room to speak privately with Les's attorney.

"I'm Lou Searing. My assistant, Jack Kelly, and I are zeroing in on crimes committed earlier today."

"I'm Steve Leonard." The attorney offered his hand, and Lou shook it.

"I'd like to talk to Les and to you, but I wanted to explain my intentions."

"Yes, that would be appreciated," Steve replied.

"If you're like me, I assume you do not like surprises."

"In my line of work, every day is a surprise."

"I can imagine. I don't know if you've heard of me, but..."

"Oh, yes, I know who you are. You have a reputation in the crime-fighting community, and in the legal arena as well. In fact, it's my pleasure to meet you."

"Thank you. I don't know what your client has told you, and I don't want to know, as that is between you and him."

"To be perfectly honest, he hasn't said much of anything," Steve replied. "It's frustrating when a judge asks you to defend someone and he looks at you like you're a stone wall."

"I'm certain you've heard of the day's events and the charges against your client."

"Yes, the FBI has provided that."

"As I said, I'd like to talk to your client, with you present. The interview will not be recorded, either by audio or visual means. I won't go into detail about what I want to ask him, but you can take all the time you need to advise him on answering my questions. Is this acceptable?"

"Not a problem. Do you want me to introduce you?"

"No, I'll do that."

Lou and Steve walked into the interrogation room where Les slouched in a chair, dressed in an orange prison jumpsuit. He looked at the floor, not making eye contact with Lou or Mr. Leonard.

"Mr. Trousard, my name is Lou Searing." Lou put out his hand for a greeting, but Les did not move. Lou sat across from Les and Steve.

"I'd like to talk with you for a few minutes. Is that okay with you?" Les remained slouched in his chair and said nothing. "I know quite a bit about you already."

Lou was silent a few seconds, and then he said, "I'm going to mention four things, and after hearing what I have to say, you may want to at least say 'hello.'

"First: on your Facebook page, you wrote, in effect, 'I'm going to see my Uncle Sam. He is about to die.' Secondly; Major Houchins is dead. Third; Shelly Westbrook is free in Winnipeg, and last, your Prime Minister has changed his mind and now supports a high-speed rail system across all of Canada."

Suddenly Les sat straight up, looked daggers at Lou, and said, "Well, I have four things to say to you, and then maybe you'll get out of here." Lou and Steve were quite surprised at the change in demeanor. This was an angry Les Trousard.

"First, who I go to see and why is none of your business. Second, I don't know anyone named Houchins. Third, Shelly Westbrook is a lying, stab-in-the-back, no-good woman, and last; of course the Prime Minister changed his mind. Wouldn't you, if you had to look over your shoulder every minute for the rest of your life?"

"Was there a conspiracy to kill the Prime Minister and the President?" Lou asked.

"Of course. Didn't you put two and two together?"

"You don't know Houchins?" Lou asked.

"If you understood conspiracy theory you'd know it's best for none of the conspirators to know of each other. That way one can't implicate the others. Maybe this Houchins was a conspirator, but he's unknown to me."

"Who saved you and Randal Beaver?" Lou asked followed by silence. "Are you expecting me to believe that you don't know the name of the man who saved your life?"

"I know who he is. Buzz Houchins, a Major in the Royal Canadian Mounted Police."

"Shelly isn't at the top of your list of favorite people, is she?" Lou asked.

"We'd have pulled it off, if not for her," Les replied.

"Can you explain?"

"I can, but I won't. It will be interesting to hear what she has to say at her trial."

"You seem like a fairly intelligent man to me," Lou said. "What did you really expect to gain by killing these two men? You had to realize that you'd either be killed or imprisoned for the rest of your life. I can't imagine a sane person doing such a thing."

"Didn't Booth think he would escape? Did Hinckley think he wouldn't be caught? We are servants of the people. They don't know what's best for them, and we need to act on their behalf!"

"You're referring to the Canadian people?" Lou asked.

"Both Americans and Canadians. A little good-for-nothing route for a high-speed rail project. If something is worth doing, it's worth doing well. Canada needed a bold vision, not some cop-out project in southern Ontario."

"So you and the others decided to take drastic action to right a wrong decision?"

"That's right."

"But you failed, Les. Your life is ruined, and for what?" Lou asked.

"I made a promise and I needed to keep it."

"Thank you for speaking with me," Lou said, rising and again offering his hand.

This time Les moved forward and shook Lou's hand. Lou walked from the room after motioning to attorney Leonard to leave with him. Once outside Lou said, "Thanks. I don't know your plan of defense, but if I were you, I'd think seriously about not guilty by reason of insanity."

Lou would share what he had heard with Jack, but for now, there was nothing more to do than wait for Carol and go home.

CHAPTER SEVENTEEN

As Carol, Lou and Jack bypassed Holland on U.S. 31, Lou's cell phone rang. Lou was driving, so he gave his phone to Carol to answer.

"Mr. Searing, please."

"He's not available at the moment. May I ask who's calling?" Carol asked.

"Please tell him Shelly Westbrook needs to talk with him."

"It's Shelly Westbrook," Carol said to Lou.

"Jack, would you take the call?" Lou asked.

Carol handed the phone to Jack. "Hi Shelly. Lou's driving, so he's asked me to speak with you."

"Hi, Jack. Have you talked to Les yet?"

"Lou has. He spoke with him in the county jail with his lawyer present."

"Did he admit to the conspiracy?"

"Yes. Said he never heard of a man named Houchins. He had little good to say about you."

"Yeah, well, consider the source. The man is insane. He's a marksman, but an insane marksman."

"Shall I ask Lou to pull off the highway so you can speak with him?"

"Yes, please. I really do need to talk to him."

Lou turned off U.S. 31, pulled into a McDonald's restaurant parking lot, and took the phone.

"Yes, Shelly."

"I wanted to explain why our conversation was interrupted. Officers of the RCMP burst into my office and arrested me for the murder of Major Houchins."

"But you said it was a suicide."

"I tried to make it look like a suicide, but I made a mistake."

"What was that?"

"I never thought they would have a surveillance camera. It was my downfall."

"I'm sorry, Shelly. You're an extremely talented journalist. Perhaps you'll become a novelist."

"Maybe. But my life is ruined."

"So, you three made up the conspiracy?" Lou asked.

"Actually, Houchins and I were the conspirators. Les was just a paid marksman. He never knew Major Houchins. I was the mastermind. I betrayed Les by telling you of his plan, and you were able to protect your President."

"So, as we approach midnight, the whole thing makes sense. Houchins has been murdered. You and Les are behind bars, with plenty of evidence to convince a jury you're guilty."

"That's a good summary," Shelly admitted.

"One more thing, Shelly. I understand the motivation to kill because of the love triangle and because of the desire to have a high-speed rail project across all of Canada, but why kill the President of the United States? It makes no sense."

Shelly began. "When Les was unsuccessful in killing Leon Abernathy, he knew he would be killed by Buzz Houchins."

"Why?" Lou asked.

"Because the evidence trail would lead back to Buzz," Shelly explained. "Les didn't fulfill his end of the bargain and the price to pay would be his life. Les thought that killing the President would lock him up in the States and that way Buzz could never get to him."

"He didn't kill the President. Buzz is dead. And now you and Les will be in prison for the rest of your lives."

"If not executed," Shelly added.

"So the only one to come out of this with his head is Buzz's brother."

"Not quite. You're forgetting about me."

"You?"

"Yes, when all is said and done, I killed the man who committed an assassination at high speed," Shelly admitted. "Just before I killed Buzz, he told me his mission had been accomplished. His exact words were, 'If Leon chewed the gum I gave him, he's dead.' Therefore, I am the one who killed the man who killed our Prime Minister. I am the one that saved the life of your President. I will live to see the sun rise and set on our beautiful Canada."

"Very shrewd, very shrewd. Good night." was all Lou said. He closed his phone and put it in his coat pocket. He shook his head, walked into McDonald's and ordered a large chocolate shake. While he waited, his cell phone rang. It was a call from the White House. He answered.

"Mr. Searing?"

"Yes."

"One moment please. The President wishes to talk with you."

A few seconds later, Lou heard President Alan Fortner's voice. "Mr. Searing. In case you have not heard, Prime Minister Abernathy is dead. He died in his sleep on a flight from Winnipeg to Ottawa. An autopsy will be performed."

"Thank you for calling."

"I just thought I owed it to you since you worked so hard with us today."

"You're well, Mr. President?" Lou asked.

"I'm fine."

"Good. My guess is the autopsy will reveal that Leon was murdered, assassinated at high speed as it were. Only time will tell if I'm right. Jack and I will send you a full report of our findings."

"Thank you. Good night, Mr. Searing."

"Good night, Mr. President."

EPILOGUE

Central Missouri was invited to join the Mid-American Conference. They accepted.

President of the United States Alan Fortner dedicated a section of his Library to the events leading up to the Victory Ride, the events that day in Michigan, and the follow-up to the high-speed rail project.

Prime Minister Leon Abernathy's autopsy revealed death by poisoning. A wad of chewing gum in his stomach was determined to be toxic.

The major traffic accident outside Durand had nothing to do with the conspiracy.

Les Trousard pled guilty to a large number of charges, from two counts of attempted murder to taking a firearm across an international border. He was sentenced to life in prison without parole.

Randal Beaver's attorney made a deal with prosecutors. Randal's cooperation and testimony against Les Trousard would allow him to avoid prosecution for assisting in an assassination by Tasering a Canadian security agent. It was Randal who placed the call warning of impending doom.

Father McGinney was released from the hospital after being treated for exhaustion and dehydration. He resumed his position, but he is assuming less responsibility in his work and taking better care of himself.

Susan Northrup, editor of the Winnipeg Free Press was questioned extensively about her role in the conspiracy and was eventually cleared as having no knowledge of the plan to kill the Prime Minister.

Shelly Westbrook was found guilty of killing Major Houchins and of conspiracy to kill the Prime Minister and the President, along with lesser charges, including illegally entering the United States. She lived to see the sun rise and set on her beloved Canada, but the day began and ended in a woman's correctional facility in western Canada. She is a model prisoner, edits the prison newspaper, and regrets her choices every day at Mass in the prison chapel.

Governor Halloran was lauded by the people of Michigan for successfully leading the state in a new long-term initiative which brought money and jobs to the Great Lakes State.

Lou Searing took a long nap the day following the Victory Ride. That evening, he and Carol walked hand in hand along the shore of Lake Michigan in front of their home. As the sun set the two gave each other a hug, thankful for one another and surviving one more investigation. Lou will eventually write a novel about the investigation as he does for every case he solves.

Jack Kelly once again enjoyed working with Lou. Elaine was thankful to have him safely home.

The high-speed rail project is on schedule. The second Victory Ride to celebrate its initial run is scheduled for Labor Day of 2017.

A MEMORY OF MY GRANDSON, LOUIS HOFFMEISTER

Lou and Nana, as Carol is known to all eight grandchildren, went to St. Louis to visit their daughter, Amanda, and her family. It was great fun to see how Hannah, Tom, Louis, and Norah were progressing. It was suggested that we all go to a golf driving range so Louis, then age 5, could be introduced to the wonderful world of golf. He seemed to know the basics of most sports; T-ball, soccer, basketball, to name a few.

We purchased a bucket of balls and walked to the end of the driving range. Of course Lou, being the patriarch golfer, had to give Louis a few pointers before realizing it was best to just let the young man try to hit the ball in whatever manner worked. Louis would have years to discover the secrets of perfect stance, swing, and club selection.

Louis stood before the ball, knees bent, and head down. He pulled the club back, and with a fluid swing, sent the ball straight down the range a good hundred yards. All of his witnesses exclaimed, "Wow!" The following shots were scattered to left and right, but an occasional shot was right on the money like his first attempt at hitting the golf ball.

Louis will have many opportunities to pursue a variety of sports: the family is quite sports-minded, and his brother Tom and sister Hannah are quite talented in their chosen athletic endeavors.

Louis's first day at the driving range gave Lou and Nana a warm feeling. It looked like the Searing tradition of enjoying golf was off to a great start. It won't be long till Louis joins his grandpa, his father, and Uncle Scott on the links. Lou hopes Louis will learn to give his grandpa long putts. He longs to hear, "Pick it up, Grandpa!"

To order additional copies of this book,
or any others written by Richard L. Baldwin,
please go to buttonwoodpress.com